DATE DUE


```
LP/WEST      Hoffman, Lee
LEE            Bred to kill
             $19.95
```

Bred To Kill

OTHER SAGEBRUSH LARGE PRINT WESTERNS BY
LEE HOFFMAN

Loco
Trouble Valley
West of Cheyenne

Bred To Kill

LEE HOFFMAN

Sagebrush
Large Print Westerns

Library of Congress Cataloging-in-Publication Data

Hoffman, Lee, 1932-
  Bred to kill / Lee Hoffman.
     p.   cm.
  ISBN 1-57490-272-5 (hardcover : alk. paper)
  1. Large type books. I. Title
  PS3558.O346 B73 2000
  813'.54—dc21   00-024594

Cataloguing in Publication Data is available from
the British Library and the National Library of Australia.

19.95

Sagebrush Large Print Westerns are published in the United
States and Canada by Thomas T. Beeler, Publisher, PO Box 659,
Hampton Falls, New Hampshire 03844-0659. ISBN 1-57490-272-5

Published in the United Kingdom, Eire, and the Republic of
South Africa by Isis Publishing Ltd, 7 Centremead, Osney
Mead, Oxford OX2 0ES England. ISBN 0-7531-6256-3

Published in Australia and New Zealand by Bolinda Publishing
Pty Ltd, 17 Mohr Street, Tullamarine, 3043, Victoria, Australia.
ISBN 1-74030-004-1

Manufactured by Sheridan Books in Chelsea, Michigan.

To Don and Jo Meisner

Bred To Kill

CHAPTER 1

"WELL NOW, I AIN'T KNOW," THE PRISONER DRAWLED. "Us Meldrins got family traditions to uphold, you know."

"You *what?*" Sheriff Glynn straightened in his swivel chair and scowled at the lean, long-boned young man sitting perched on the edge of his desk. Even with the flame of the coal-oil lamp reflected in them, Meldrin's eyes seemed as flat and expressionless as a plank wall.

Reaching up, one hand dragging the other at the end of the short-chain handcuffs, Meldrin pushed back his hat. Hair the color of a dirty claybank hung wetly on his forehead. He brushed at it with his knuckles. His grin was lopsided, still a little drunken, as he answered the sheriff. "First Meldrin in this here country was sent over from England as a convict back when they was sold for slaves to the colonies. You didn't know that, did you, Glynn? You didn't know us Meldrins was fine old first settlers like that?" He paused, looking as if he expected an answer.

Glynn shook his head slowly.

"Great-Grandpappy Robert, he was the first man to be hanged for horse-thieving in Ware County. Us Meldrins was first at a lot of things. Grandpappy Robert, oldest boy always got named Robert, he was quite a feller. He was the first man in Georgia to—well, he never got caught. And my own pappy, he got the family run out of Georgia back in '58."

"He didn't stop at that," Glynn said.

"Hell, no! You know yourself how it was with Pap and my brothers and me. We rode hell out'n that

1

Kansas-Missouri line all through the war and after. They wasn't so many of us like they was with Quantrill or Lane or Jennison, but we done well enough for ourselves. I reckon if we was still together we'd of come close onto making Meldrin as big a name as James or Younger."

"But you ain't all together anymore," the sheriff snapped at him. "You're all either dead or in jail."

"I ain't *exactly* in jail."

"You ain't exactly out of it either!"

Meldrin grimaced. "Now Glynn, you know damn well I ain't stole that dun horse. I *paid* for it, nigh every cent I had. And I got papers to prove it. But that jackrabbit deputy of your'n, he wouldn't even look at them. He just up and hauled me in here—like I was a *thief* or something. That ain't no way for a lawman to act, is it, Sheriff?" He gave Glynn a doleful look as he dug into a vest pocket. Awkwardly because of the handcuffs, he fished out a plug of Daniel Webster. Dusting off the lint, he took a bite, and stuffed the plug back into his pocket.

As he worked the tobacco between his jaws, he picked up the deputy sheriff's badge that lay on the desk and turned it between his fingers, studying it.

Wordlessly Glynn watched him and wondered whether he'd been mistaken. Maybe it was too late. Maybe Clant Meldrin was beyond reasoning with.

Meldrin let fly a spate of tobacco juice at the brass cuspidor by the desk and wiped his mouth with his knuckles. "Glynn," he said, "you *serious* about this?"

"Damn serious."

"You ain't make sense to me."

"Are you interested?" the sheriff asked him.

He squinted at the star and frowned critically. "You,

2

reckon wearing this thing would keep me out'n jail for a while?" he asked.

Glynn shook his head. "Only thing'll ever keep you out of jail is you learn to behave yourself and respect the law. Quit throwing your fist at anybody that calls you by name and learn yourself to do a day's work for your wage. You do that and you'll be able to stay out of trouble."

With a snort, Meldrin tossed the badge down on the desk. "Ain't what I *do* gets me into trouble. It's who I am."

"What do you mean by that?"

Scrubbing a hand over the stubble on his jaw, Meldrin answered thoughtfully, "Being Clant Meldrin is nigh a hanging offense by itself in some parts of this country. Rest of the parts, it's enough to get me accused of damn near anything what happens. And even of things what ain't happen—like somebody stealing that dun horse."

The sheriff picked up a pencil and leaned back in his chair. He tugged at the ends of the pencil with both hands. "I know you didn't steal that horse, Clant. I just wanted to talk to you, quiet and peaceable. When I sent Johnny to fetch you out'n the saloon, I told him he could use the horse as an excuse, but only if you wouldn't come along and talk sociable without he had to use force."

"If you know I ain't stole that horse, what you got me in irons for?" Meldrin jerked at the chain between his wrists.

"For trying to put your knuckles down Johnny's throat when he went to give you my invite. You hadn't no call to do that."

"He hadn't no call to come up behind me like he done

3

and sudden tap me on the shoulder. Not just when I was about to start swinging on some other feller," he protested. "He should have seen I wasn't sober enough to care who I was hitting."

"Are you sober enough now to talk sense?" Glynn asked.

"I reckon. You damn near drownded me in that horse trough. Do you get a bonus from the county or something if you drown me, Sheriff?"

"Right now I'd be tempted to pay for the privilege," the lawman sighed. "Look here, Clant. You interested or ain't you?"

Meldrin grinned again. "S'pose I was to do it? S'pose I was to up and disgrace the family name by taking work with the law? What would be in it for me?"

The sheriff tapped the point of the pencil against his teeth. "Maybe not much. Depends on how you look at it. It's honest work and there's wages goes with it. You take the job, do it, and behave yourself, you'll have money in your pocket, food in your belly, and a warm bed."

Meldrin mocked a scowl of surprise. "You're asking me to break with all my family traditions just for wages and found?"

"Dammit, Clant, I'm not playing games. I'm offering you a good job. You answer me, will you? You want it or not?"

"'What the hell ever give you the notion I might want a good job?"

"You got paid off from the Box T this morning. It's coming winter and it gets right cold in this here part of the territory. A dollar a day and board is a damn sight better'n riding grubline in the snow."

"Thirty and found!"

4

"You've worked for that. You worked six weeks out at the Tatum spread for it. And you've worked for less."

"I ain't worked very hard for it, though."

"You damn well ain't. What's it been now, Clant? Close onto two years, ain't it, since you got out of the penitentiary? How many jobs you had in that time? Three, four days in one place, maybe a week or two at the next?"

"How come you know what I been doing these past two years?"

"I know you've been wearing the seat out'n your britches working at near onto any kind of job you can do off the back of a horse, and I know you ain't been able to hold a job for more'n a few weeks at the most. You've just drifted around. Last year you wintered in south Texas, hanging around with a bunch of no-accounts that could get you back into real trouble as quick as you can do it yourself. I know that you come north again this spring droving with a beef herd, only you didn't even got as far as the railhead—"

"I got run out!" he protested. "Them folks in Kansas is a mite touchy about us Meldrins. They didn't even give me till sundown to get back across the line."

"And then you headed over this way—"

"Hell, they didn't even give me a chance to collect my time."

Glynn persisted. "I know you worked close onto three weeks at Gil Nash's spread across the Home River before you got busted there. Then you come over to this side and stuck it out at Tatum's for all of six weeks, which is likely a record for you. But now you're out again and it's coming winter. Clant, you ain't got a chance of finding riding work around here this time of year. What I'm offering you is an honest job that'll keep

5

you warm and fed through the winter. Likely, it's the best chance you'll ever come onto. But all you'll do is just sit there and make mock of me."

"How come you know so damn much about what I been doing?" Meldrin demanded again.

"Never you mind how I know. It's enough I know you've been in and out of jobs and in and out of jails and even run out of towns for close onto two years now. Ain't you tired of that kind of life yet? Or you got a notion that's how you want to go on for the rest of your days?"

Meldrin was gazing down at the star again. When he spoke, his voice was so low that the sheriff could barely make out the words. "It's been ten years now since the end of the war, but the Rebs still hate the Union and the Blue-Bellies still hate the Secesh. And ain't hardly nobody got no use for a border guerrilla."

"You claim that's your trouble, Clant? You got a label hung on you back when you was a kid and folks still keep reading it? You claim now you're just a nice, peaceable, law-abiding citizen but wherever you go you get give a hard time on account of you're a Meldrin?"

"I'll tell you the truth of it," Clant said softly, running a finger along the badge where it lay on the desk. "I get me a job tending beeves and there I am callusing up my hands and my butt chasing cows out the bushes and cleaning water holes and unkinking half-broke horses before breakfast and just plain minding my own business, except wherever I go they comes along somebody what is from Kansas or maybe Missouri or what had kin there. Or maybe he ain't but only *read* in the newspapers about how it was back during the troubled times.

"Well, he's got him a family or an uncle or maybe it

6

was a fifth cousin three times removed what got burnt out by the Border Roughs. Or maybe he only *read* about folks getting burnt out and robbed by the raiders. Maybe it was Quantrill or Jennison or Anderson, or maybe the Meldrins, what done it. Or maybe it was done under Order Eleven, or even by Billy Sherman and his Bummers on their way through Georgia. That don't make him no never mind. He just comes up to me and says, 'So you're Clant Meldrin.'

"Maybe I take a poke at him then. Or maybe we hold off and just look mean at each other for a few days. But always they comes a time I bust a couple of his teeth loose. Or he tries to push mine down my gullet. Then the ramrod comes along and he says to me, 'Meldrin, the boss'd like to see you inside.'

"I go on into the office with my hat in my hands and my head down like he was the warden and he kind of gees and haws a mite and says to me how he was some kind of officer under some damned major or general on one side or the other, but he has put all that behind him. Then he says, 'Meldrin, I have tried to be fair with you and I don't hold none of the things your family done again' you, you understand? And I says, 'Yessir,' quiet and nice, like he was a goddammed warden, and he says, 'Well, you know yourself, Meldrin, you ain't no top hand. You can't throw a rope worth a damn and half the time you get a calf down, it gets away from you,' and things like that. And I says, 'Yessir.' Then he says, 'Well, that feller out there what you just tried to bust the jaw on, he is a top hand and that's what I need on this spread, Meldrin. And it surely looks like you and him just can't work, together. You understand that, Meldrin? And nice and polite, like I was answering the warden, I says, 'Yessir.' So he gives me my time."

7

"That how it went at the Box T?" Glynn asked.

"Tatum weren't the only one. I've heard about the same elsewheres plenty enough."

"Well, maybe you *ain't* a top hand. Maybe you ain't been good enough to hold them jobs. You ever consider that?"

Clant nodded. "It's true enough, I reckon. I ain't very good with beeves." He pushed the shackle up on his right arm and rubbed at the old ragged scars that circled the joint of his wrist. "I surely can't set a rope nowheres near where I want it."

"The job I'm offering you don't call for roping. All you got to do is use your head and hold your temper."

"And do what I'm told?"

"You'll find that on any job you get, Clant. It ain't that folks are trying to boss you around, the way you think. It's just the way things work out in this world. Somebody's got to ramrod, got to plan and organize things, or they don't get done. Same way with an honest job as it is with horse-thieving and bank-robbing. A man's got to take orders."

"I reckon I've took a fair piece of 'em in my time," Clant muttered. "I ain't hardly ever done nothing else but."

"Are you interested?" Glynn asked him again.

He frowned. He looked as if he were giving the proposal serious consideration.

The sheriff put down the pencil and leaned back in his chair, waiting for an answer. Outside he could hear the drum of a beginning rain on the awning over the plank walk. A good thing, he thought. It would lay the dust that was still thick on the roads.

Meldrin looked up. "Glynn?" he said, and the sheriff straightened in his chair, anxious for an answer. "Glynn,

8

you reckon I could sleep in the jailhouse tonight? I mean with the door open."

Glynn slumped back. With an edge of disgust in his voice, he asked, "Where had you figured on sleeping?"

"I ain't know. I'd have found me a place."

"You collected your time when you were fired this morning, didn't you?"

"I kind of spent most of it. I paid a right high price for that horse you hauled me in for the stealing of."

"You broke yourself buying a horse?"

Meldrin nodded. "He's a real good horse. I figured as how I might ought to head south again before the snows start. But I ain't much for walking and Dog, he ain't so good at catching them boxcars."

"You got *any* money left?" Glynn asked.

"Two bits."

"That's all you got?"

"Hell, no!" He counted on his fingers, one-handed, using his thumb to mark against the joints. "I got me a real good horse, a saddle with a fair-decent Spencer in the boot, a heavy wool shirt, a slicker and a short coat, a cap-and-ball Remington in my war bag, and the clothes I'm wearing. And two bits hard money. That ain't so bad. Better'n I had two year ago."

"And a hungry mongrel dog" Glynn added to complete the inventory.

"Dog ain't *belong* to me," Meldrin said. "We just kind of happen to be traveling together." He paused; then he asked, "You reckon if I'm gonna sleep in the jail, maybe you could let Dog in too? It sounds to be getting a mite cold and wet out there."

"What about the horse? You want *him* in too?"

"Well now, I figured you'd be putting him in the stable on the county bill, Sheriff. Leastways till you can

9

check with Tatum tomorrow and find out for sure whether he's stole property."

"Goddammit, Clant!" Glynn started. He stopped himself. Easing wearily back into the chair, he mumbled it under his breath. "Goddammit—"

"You got a charge again' me, Sheriff?" Meldrin asked innocently.

He held out his hands. "Then how 'bout you take these irons off me?"

Moving slowly, as if he were burdened by some heavy weight, Glynn dug out the key and unlocked the handcuffs. As he pulled them off, his eyes held to the scars on Meldrin's wrist. With a sigh, he said, "Go fetch your dog. And help yourself to a cell."

CHAPTER 2

CLANT MELDRIN LAY SPRAWLED ON THE CELL BUNK with his hat over his face. He listened to the rain that had been falling all night and still came down in a thin drizzle. From the sound of it and the feel of the damp, chill air, traveling wasn't going to be any too pleasant. Especially not on horseback.

Under the hand he dangled over the edge of the bunk, he felt the big scruffy dog stir slightly. The dog raised his head and Meldrin heard the soft, low growl deep in his throat.

"Mornin, Sheriff," he said, not moving, but listening to the footsteps coming into the back room of the jailhouse.

For a big man, Glynn walked softly. But then his build wasn't of the fat, clumsy type. It was all bone and hard meat, and he carried himself as if he was used to

10

spending a lot more time in the saddle than in that swivel chair. He was the kind, Clant had decided, who would push his quarry right up to the county line—and a little over if he thought he could make his catch. A hard man to have on your trail.

Suddenly he sat bolt upright, shouting, "What the hell is that for?" Glynn had slammed the barred door shut.

The sheriff took his time. He spun himself a quirly, stuck it in his face, and lit it as Meldrin watched. He took a deep drag and let the smoke out through his nose. Finally, he answered, "I told Shorty down to the café to send over breakfast for a prisoner. I ain't of a mind to have to explain why the county is buying meals for a prisoner it ain't got shut in."

"Oh," Meldrin grunted. "Then you ain't figure on locking that door?"

"No." Glynn eyed him and said, "You don't much like having a door shut on you, do you? You don't like it at all, being in a jail?"

Meldrin hooked his heels over the frame of the bed and rested his arms on his knees. Leaning his head back against the wall, he looked at the sheriff from under half-closed lids. "Is they anybody *likes* it?"

"You ought to be used to it by now."

"It ain't a thing a man *gets* used to."

"And the penitentiary? In four years did you get used to that?"

Clant fingered the plug out of his pocket and bit off a chunk. He worked the quid a couple of times; then he tucked it into his cheek and said, "Sheriff, I ain't sure as how breakfast is worth the work of listening to you talk."

Ignoring the remark, Glynn asked, "The way you're living now, Clant—how long you reckon you'll be able

11

to last it out?"

"Huh?"

"How long you reckon it'll be before you get tired of drifting hungry and decide to throw in with some of your no-account friends to make the kind of trouble that will end you up back in the penitentiary?"

Meldrin's gaze was narrow and suspicious. "I ain't going back," he said flatly.

"You're sure as hell headed that way. And you ain't half-growed kid no more. Ain't any judge going to go easy on you the next time."

He drew breath sharply. "Look here, Glynn. I ain't killed nobody since I was a young 'un and I ain't got no plans in that direction. I ain't even carry my gun on my hip no more. But anybody tries to send me back there again, he's gonna see himself one goddamn massacre like nobody ever—" He cut himself short, realizing that he was shouting and surprised at what he was saying. He meant it sure enough, but what kind of a damn fool was he to holler it out that way—and at a lawman to boot?

Easing the tension in his shoulders, he leaned back against the wall again. Outside, he heard a door slam and a voice call for the sheriff.

Glynn answered and the kid from the café came into the room with a tray. He glanced curiously at Meldrin as he gave it to the sheriff. Glynn ignored the curiosity in his face and sent him on his way. Then he opened the cell door and gave the tray to Meldrin.

Shifting his legs crossways, Indian-fashion, Clant settled the tray between his knees. He took a deep whiff of the warm aroma of ham, eggs, and biscuits, and began hacking at the meat. He stabbed one chunk on the tip of the knife and held it down. The dog took it gently

12

between his teeth and Clant jabbed another piece of meat for himself. Then he divvied up the eggs.

"You always share with that animal?" Glynn asked.

"Dog here?" Meldrin looked up. "He generally fetches for himself. But all the game you got in this here jail is rats and chinches and they ain't fit eating. Not for no self-respecting dog."

Glynn grinned a bit to himself. Maybe now that he was sober, Meldrin would show a little more sense than he had the night before. He asked, "Clant, you give any more thought to that offer I made you last night?"

Meldrin mumbled something in reply through a mouthful of biscuit, gulped at the coffee, and then said it again; "You really make me that offer? I had a notion that was some fool idea I got out'n a bottle."

"It was real," Glynn told him.

He wiped at his mouth with the back of his hand. "What's the trick to it?"

"No trick. I'm just offering you a job as a deputy to me."

"*Me*?"

The sheriff nodded.

"You expecting some kind of trouble that'll get your hired help killed off or something?"

"No trick, Clant. It's the same job I'd be offering to any man I wanted for a deputy. Happens I'm offering it to you."

"Maybe you're trying to throw the next election and you're looking for some easy way to get real unpopular around the county fast," Meldrin speculated.

"Dammit, Clant!" Glynn started, but he caught rein on his tongue and busied himself building another smoke as he cast about in his mind for some way of making an explanation that Clant Meldrin would find

13

acceptable. He sure as hell couldn't tell him the truth. Finally, he said, "Clant, fact is I got a problem that you might could be a lot of help to me with."

"Oh?" He put down the empty tray and leaned his head against the wall again. Thumbing the Daniel Webster out of his pocket, he bit off about half of what was left of it, then he asked curiously, "What you need help with, Sheriff?"

"It's Paul Fairweather."

"Ol' Texas Paul? How come him to be a problem to you?"

"He's here in the county."

"What give you that notion?"

"A couple of days ago one of the Jay-Bar riders was hunting strays up on the side of Bloodyhead Mountain. He spotted sign of some men having made a cold camp and then having moved on up into the Stove Rocks. It got him curious and he kept his eyes open. Next day he got a look at a couple of riders. A real good look. This Jay-Bar cowboy is a Texan himself, and he's seen Fairweather down there. He recognized him."

"What would Texas Paul be doing up there?" Meldrin asked.

"From the sign that Jay-Bar boy seen, he's holed up with some of his men, maybe gathering more. Either he's figuring on wintering up there or he's got some kind of plans that brought him this way. Winter comes damn cold and hard up on Bloodyhead and it ain't no place to spend the season. But Jubilee here has growed into a fairsize town, since the railroad come through and sometimes there's a good piece of cash in the town. I figure it could be that Fairweather's up there making plans for some of it."

"You expecting to have a good piece of cash money

14

in town sometime soon?" Meldrin asked. When Glynn hesitated in answering, he grinned and said, "Ne'mind. I got no notion of busting open no banks around here. Not by my lonesome, I ain't."

"It ain't that, Clant," Glynn mumbled.

"Like hell it ain't."

"Look here, I don't think you want the kind of trouble getting mixed up in a bank robbery would get you. Do you think I'd offer you this job if—?"

"Ne'mind," Clant said again. He worked the quid between his jaws and spat into the pot in the corner of the cell. "Just what is it you reckon *I* could do about Texas Paul?"

"I know you were friendly with him down in Texas. I know you got a fair knowledge of his kind of operation. I figure maybe you could find out what he's holed up in the Stove Rocks for."

"You want me to kind of mosey up and ask him what his plans are and then turn 'round and come back and tell you what he answers me? I can tell you right now what his answer to any fool thing like that'd be—six kicks of one of these fancy new Colt revolvers."

"That ain't what I mean," Glynn said. He settled himself into the straight-back chair outside the cell and as he talked he tilted it back onto its hind legs. "Fact is, Clant, I figure anybody who goes up too far into the Stove Rocks while Fairweather and his crew are there had better be fair nervy and damn handy with a gun. I reckon you're both."

"Me? Why I'm a real peaceable man, Sheriff," Meldrin drawled. "I got me an old handgun tucked away in my war bag, but I ain't even know if it'll work or not."

"Funny thing," Glynn mocked his drawl, "I was

15

talkin' to Bill Langer over to the mercantile a while back and he mentioned the shopping you'd been doing there. Seems real curious how a man could have spent as much of his wage on powder and pig as you've done and still not even know if his gun's fit to shoot."

"Me?" Meldrin looked at him, wide-eyed and innocent.

"Tell me, Clant, when Tatum'd send you up to Deer Creek Meadow hunting strays—you find much wandering beef just lazing around throwing lead at jackrabbits?"

Meldrin shrugged. "I reckon I got a mite curious could I still hit anything with a handgun. I kinda got out of practice for a while there."

"You've kinda got back into practice these past couple of years too, ain't you? You've got a real fast hand."

"Guns is about the only thing I was ever very good at," he muttered. "Pap wouldn't never let me ride along till I got to where I could hit a mark and fire off a Navy without it kicked me off'n my horse. I learnt quick though."

"Ever occur to you that if you was to put as much time and study into working cows as you've done into throwing a gun, you might get good at that too?"

"I never give it no thought."

"You ever think about anything? You ever *try* learning anything besides guns?"

Meldrin's shoulders jerked as if he had started to move but caught rein on himself. He took a deep breath; then he opened his hands and held them out in front of him. Looking at them critically, he said, "Cowboying is kind of a two-handed trade."

"What do you mean by that?"

16

Flexing the fingers of his right hand, he gazed at it. "I ain't exactly got two hands, Glynn. *You* know that."

The sheriff frowned. It hadn't occurred to him. He thought back to the times when he'd gone sneaking up to the Deer Creek Meadow with the purpose of watching Clant from the cover of the brush. He'd never seen him favor the hand in any way—not when he was molding shot or loading the old revolver. It just hadn't occurred to him that Clant might have trouble with his hand.

As he opened and closed his fingers, Meldrin added, "I ain't very handy with this one."

Glynn told him, "I never seen you have no trouble with it. And my deputy says you throw punches with it real well."

He clenched the fist. "Hitting works from the shoulder, not the wrist."

"Ever have any trouble saddling a horse or cleaning a gun?"

"Are you trying to make me out a liar, Sheriff?"

"Just wondering."

"Damn Box T ramrod kept wondering the same way."

"Maybe he had reason to wonder."

"Truth is, it's kinda sometimesy," he admitted. "I get me holt of some slick-eared calf and start trying to pig a string around its legs or I try heaving a hayfork or I set out to put stitches back into a piece of harness, sometimes I can do it all right. But sometimes I just ain't got no grip at all, nor I can't get my fingers to go where I want them."

You mean if it's honest work—Glynn stopped himself from saying it. He had a feeling it wouldn't do any good and would just rile Clant. He decided maybe some different line of argument would be wiser. "While back

I knew a feller name of Sam Trot who lost his whole arm off right up to here back in the war." He touched his shoulder. "Sam was a drover. Got top wages and he earned 'em, too. It don't always take two hands to work a good cowhorse or sing a night herd to sleep. Not for a man who really puts his mind to doing the job."

Meldrin stood up and stretched his shoulders. Yawning, he leaned against the doorframe and looked at the sheriff. "You know, Glynn, you're about the talkin'est man I ever run onto. You set me in mind of them fellers what used to come around the prison to fetch us poor convicts salvation. I recall they was times when I up and got myself into trouble apurpose just so's I wouldn't have to set and listen to 'em. Lordy, they could pure talk the ears off a jackass."

"I don't see where they shortened yours any, Meldrin."

The move was sudden. Almost before he had closed his mouth on the last word, almost before he could realize what was happening, Glynn felt the hard bone of knuckle slam into his face. The blow jerked his head back and he felt the chair tipping. He fell hard as it went over. Rolling he tried to get up but one foot had gone through the rungs and he found himself tangled in the chair. Bracing his elbow, he propped himself up and looked at Clant Meldrin. "You're a mite proddy, aint you?" he said, rubbing his jaw with his free hand.

"You gonna get up?" Meldrin snapped at him.

"You figure to knock me down again?"

"Yeah."

"I don't want to fight you, Clant."

"They ain't many that does. Not after they've tried it."

"Dammit," Glynn muttered. He looked at Meldrin's

18

clenched fists. He'd seen the right hand dart into a pocket, but whatever he had in it was hidden under his fingers.

"You gonna get up?"

Glynn drew a deep breath and let it out with a sigh, but he made no move to rise.

"I've give you fair chance at me," Meldrin said. "If you ain't want it, I'm willing to beat hell out'n you while you're down."

"What you got in your hand, Clant?"

The question seemed to surprise him. He looked at his hand as if it were news to him and opened the fingers slightly. "Iron," he said.

Glynn could see the stubby section of a railroad spike that he held. "You figure that's honest fighting?"

"Makes up a mite for the strength I ain't got in that wrist," Meldrin answered him. "And I ain't much like fighting when I get beat. You got a good twenty pound on me, Sheriff. You gonna stand up and fight or you want me to kick your ribs in?"

Glynn sighed again. Carefully, he disentangled his foot from the chair, and slowly he stood up.

Meldrin lunged at him.

The sheriff's hand was fast. When he brought it up, he had his long-barreled Colt in it. He swung, laying the gun along Meldrin's jaw, sending him sprawling back against the bars of the cell.

It took Clant a good piece of a minute to get his eyes focused again. When he did, he found himself looking into the muzzle of the colt.

"I don't want to fight you, Clant," Glynn said again.

"I reckon not," Meldrin agreed as he studied on the gun. "You figure on locking me up or running me out?"

Glynn looked as if he'd reached the bitter end of his

19

throw rope. Coldly, he said, "Got a preference?"

"I'd as leave get moving before the snow starts," Clant answered. He felt the nudge of Dog's nose at his ribs. Slowly, keeping his eyes steady on the gun, he reached out a hand and roughed his fingers into the thick hair of the dog's neck.

Glynn almost snapped out for him to get going. But he held up and considered a moment. He couldn't just give up and let Clant go. Not like this. "No, I ain't through with you yet. Get back into that cell."

Clant rubbed his knuckles along his jaw. "What do you mean, you *ain't through* with me?"

"What I said. Get back in that cell," the sheriff gave a jerk of his head. He raised the hand with the gun in it, as if he meant to swing it again.

With a shrug of resignation, Clant took hold of the bars and pulled himself up onto his feet. He stepped back into the cell, with the dog close at his heels. Behind him, he heard Glynn slam the door shut. He settled onto the bunk and watched as this time the sheriff turned the key in the lock. He could feel the icy chill the sound of the tumblers sent down his spine. It wasn't a thing a man ever got used to.

The dog lay his big head on Clant's knees, and he sunk his fingers into the neck hair again. Dog just plain didn't understand about being locked in. It didn't seem to make a damn bit of difference to him.

"Dog," he mumbled, "How come you'll eat my food but you won't never jump nobody for me? You'd join in the fight now and then, you could do me a damn lot, of good."

"Clant," Glynn said.

Meldrin made a pass at the dog with his open hand and the animal grabbed at him, getting the hand between his teeth. Bearing down gently, Dog made a happy growling deep in his throat. At least with Dog here, Clant wasn't locked in alone.

"Clant," the sheriff repeated.

When Meldrin finally looked up at him, it was to ask a question. "How long you figure to hold me here?"

Glynn snapped back, "How come you swung on me that way?"

He considered. It was in his face that he wasn't too sure himself. He said, "I ain't like the way you said my name."

"You and your goddamn name," Glynn muttered. "You got a notion you're hell on flanged wheels, ain't you, Clant? You figure when you walk down the street everybody's pointing at your back and speaking your name in whispers. You got a notion when kids are bad their folks tell 'em to behave or Clant Meldrin will get them. You think the name of Meldrin gives folks fits of terror."

"'It damn well did back during the war!"

"What do you know about the war? You were a miserable snot-nosed kid during the war."

"I rode the last year or so!" Clant shouted at him. "And I rode every damned time after it!"

"Proud of it, ain't you? Proud of it and damned by it," Glynn snapped back. "Well, I'll tell you, Clant, there's a mess of people in this town who never even heard the name of Meldrin. Or if they did, it wasn't until after you signed on at the Box T and started making trouble around these parts. You think they hold it again' you, what your family did during the war? Sure, the ones what come from around the Kansas-Missouri line likely remember the name of Meldrin well enough, and there's a lot of 'em will hate you for it. But they're damn far

21

from being all the people there is in this country. Acting the way you do, you ask for trouble. Then you blame it on your name being Meldrin. If you *wanted* different— if you acted different—wouldn't hardly anybody think anything more about you than if your name was Jones or Smith or Johnson. You got sense enough to understand that?" He stopped talking and waited for some response. But he got none.

Meldrin worked his hand from between the dog's teeth and dug his fingers into the scruff of the dog's neck. This seemed to occupy all of his attention, as if somehow he'd slammed a solid door between himself and the sheriff and was no longer aware of Glynn's presence. He roughed the dog's big head between both hands.

Glynn waited. Finally, feeling a dull sense of frustration, he turned and walked back into the office. He slumped himself down into the swivel chair and picked up a fistful of the papers that were scattered over the desk. Forcing thoughts of Clant Meldrin out of his mind, he thumbed through them. It had gotten to the point where there was too damned much paperwork involved in sheriffing. And the way Jubilee had grown since the railroad had come through, it was damned well time the town got itself a lawman instead of depending on the county for its peacekeeping. Johnny Ward should have been in the office, taking care of most of the paperwork, instead of out tending chores that rightly belonged to a town marshal.

He squirmed in the chair, feeling uncomfortable no matter how he shifted around. He had a longing to be on his horse, somewhere well out of the town and away from all this damned paperwork that plagued him. Away from—Damn Clant Meldrin. Trying to talk sense to him was like arguing with an Arkansas jack. Maybe the only way to put a little sense into his head would be to pound it in.

No, he told himself, that didn't seem like a very promising idea either. If Clant hadn't gotten any sense beaten into him during four years in the penitentiary, one more beating wasn't likely to do the job.

Glynn shook his head slowly. He couldn't see any promising way to approach Clant Meldrin. But he couldn't give up either.

CHAPTER 3

GLYNN SHUFFLED THE PAPERS AND THEN THREW THEM down. Just as he had leaned back in the chair and was starting to swing his feet up onto the desk he heard Meldrin call out.

With a sigh, he got up and stuck his head through the doorway. "What is it now?"

Meldrin was stretched out on the bunk with his hands under his head. He didn't look around as he asked, "Stopped raining, ain't it, Sheriff?"

"Look out the window and see."

Still not moving, he said, "I run out'n tobacco."

"So?"

"I ain't much of a mind of lie around your jailhouse without I got no tobacco," he answered. Propping himself up on one elbow, he looked at the sheriff. "If it's stopped raining, I reckon I might as well ride on up toward them Stove Rocks and take that look around for you."

Glynn grinned. He felt a vague kind of relief and pleasure, even if the victory did seem a small and tentative one. As he unlocked the door, he asked, "You know where the Stove Rocks is?"

Meldrin nodded. "Tatum's beef range's up that way. I've rode the ground a time or two."

"It's better'n a day's travel from here," Glynn said, leading him into the office. "I'll give you a note to Bill Langer for supplies against the county bill. And release to the stable for your horse. You want to leave the dog here?"

"I ain't never tell Dog what to do. He can come or stay as he chooses," Meldrin answered. "If I run into Texas Paul, you want me to give him any particular message from you?"

The sheriff leaned a hand on the desk as he scribbled out the notes. "You can tell him it gets pretty damn cold up there and he'd do better to move himself out'n this part of the country before the snow sets in."

"Sounds like pretty good advice," Meldrin muttered. He took the notes and scanned them. "You ain't say here how much credit I can get at the mercantile."

"You figure for yourself what supplies you'll need. It should take you about three days to get there and back. Add on at least another day or two for looking around." Glynn eyed him askance. "Or maybe you're thinking of supplies enough to get you back to Texas?"

Clant folded the notes carefully and tucked them into a pocket. "I'm thinking about Dan'l Webster, Sheriff. I get right lonesome without him and I ain't got but two bits cash money of my own."

"Get your tobacco. I'll charge it against your wage. As long as you're working for me." Glynn jerked open the desk drawer and pulled out the deputy's star. As Clant picked it up, he added, "You got an oath to swear."

24

Clant nodded. He swore the oath as the sheriff read it and pocketed the badge. As he started toward the door, Glynn called after him, "You *are* coming back, ain't you?"

Clant shot him a quick grin and walked out with the dog close at his heels.

For a long moment, Glynn stood looking at the doorway and wondering. A week, he figured. If Clant wasn't back within a week it'd likely mean he'd taken and lit a shuck southward. If he did that, what then?

He shook his head slowly. Had he done the wrong thing again? Had he just given Clant the easy way again—the chance to run instead of facing up to the world?

And if Clant did run—Glynn had the desperate feeling that this was his own last chance. If Clant ran, it was likely he'd never come back this way again. At least not on any honest business.

He lowered himself into the swivel chair and picked up the papers, but he couldn't focus his attention on them. The sense of responsibility gnawed at his thoughts like a rat.

He was still staring at the papers, still not really seeing them, when a shadow crossed the doorway. He looked up and smiled. Nora Ellison was a handsome woman and a welcome sight.

She stepped into the office, looking like a picture out of a catalogue. The bonnet she wore wasn't big enough to keep the sun off her face but it made a perfect frame for her features, and the little blue flowers on it were just the right color to go with her dark chestnut hair and amber eyes. The plain woolen dress was of a darker shade of the same blue, with traces of white lace around the throat.

25

But then Nora always made a perfect picture. She'd explained to him once how it was good business for a seamstress to be well dressed.

"Morning, Nora," he said, rising to his feet.

She was frowning slightly as she asked, "Wasn't that Clant Meldrin I just saw leaving?"

He nodded.

"What did he do?" she asked.

Glynn pulled the Windsor chair out from the wall a bit for her, thinking quickly. He couldn't recall ever having told her about Clant. The occasion hadn't come up and it wasn't something he fancied talking about. It was too much like showing a sore on his conscience that had never quite healed. He wondered if he should tell her now, or if he should keep it to himself.

"He asked me last night if he could sleep here, out'n the rain," he said. Talking to Nora had always been easy. He had always been able to speak the things he truly felt to her without the feeling that he was betraying weakness in himself. And it had eased his mind to share thoughts with her, especially the ones that had troubled him. That was the way it should be between a man and the woman he planned to marry. He decided to tell it all to her, from the beginning.

"Mary Tatum was in for a fitting yesterday," she was saying. "She told me that they finally fired Meldrin. She said it was really a relief to have him off the place. None of the hands could get along with him."

"Why not?" he asked. "Did she say what the trouble was?"

"He got into a fight with the new man they—"

"No, I know about that. I mean, did Mrs. Tatum say why none of the regular hands could get along with him?"

"She said the boys were of the opinion he never earned his wage and they resented it. And he skulked around acting like he was looking for trouble, like he was primed to explode at the least touch. Mary said he was a born troublemaker. I suppose they're well rid of him. You will be, too, Lamar. Jubilee doesn't need that kind. From what I've heard about him—"

"Nora." He said it so solemnly that she stopped short and gazed at him.

"What's the matter, Lamar?" she asked gently.

He seated himself on the edge of the desk and picked up a pencil. "Honey, I've offered Clant a job as my deputy."

"Lamar! That man's an outlaw. The stories I've heard since he came here—"

"He served his time."

"He's a killer, Lamar. You're from Missouri yourself. You know about the Meldrins."

"I know Clant Meldrin," he said. "Least I knew him about as well as any did back there. We grew up hunting the same woods back in Jackson County."

She looked at him with puzzled concern.

He turned the pencil in his fingers, wondering just where to start. "The Meldrin bunch moved into Jackson back around '58," he told her. "It was the old man and seven boys. I think they come to Jackson so's they could get in on the border trouble and profit by it. That was the kind they was.

"They put up a shack 'way back in the woods and made some sign of clearing and putting in crops, but it was only a sign. Meldrins never took their living out of the ground. It was horses they specialized in—other folks' horses. They'd take hogs and beeves and anything else they could lay their hands on without they

27

got caught, but mostly they traded in horses.

"I used to run onto one or another of the boys once in a while when I was out hunting, but I can't say I exactly ever knew none of them. The older ones carried guns and the young 'uns threw rocks, and none was very sociable toward strangers. They were a rough bunch. Never went into town but what some of 'em would get into a fight of some kind. Just for the fun of it, it seemed like. And never one of 'em went into town alone where he could get ganged up on and jumped."

He stopped talking long enough to roll a smoke and get it fired. "I recall it was the summer I turned sixteen that I come onto Clant.

"We'd been losing eggs nigh every night and sometimes chickens too, and Paw figured it wasn't a varmint getting them on account there wasn't any bloody feathers or busted eggshells. He figured it was a Meldrin, but try as he might he couldn't fetch up on the thief. So finally he decided to set a trap. A wolf trap."

"A wolf trap!" she repeated incredulously.

He nodded.

"But that's a terrible thing!"

"It is," he agreed. "Paw must have figured so, too, else he wouldn't have talked to excuse himself as much as he did. It was an old trap that was bent a bit so the jaws didn't quite close, but the spring was strong enough. He kept saying how it wouldn't do no real damage and then he'd say how the Meldrin boys was being raised like a bunch of wild animals and the best thing could happen to any of them would be to get caught thieving and sent off to some proper institution where he'd get taught right.

"Paw'd say how boys was like colts. Catch 'em young enough and train 'em right, they could be good

28

pullers. He said if the Meldrin boys could be caught young and taught civilized ways, they could be turned into decent citizens." He looked at her intently and asked, "You reckon that's so?"

"I never thought about it."

"Well, I've thought about it. On an' off all these years I've thought about it. Every time I got word of the Meldrins' hell-raising I thought about it." He snubbed out the quirly and got to his feet. Then he sat down on the edge of the desk again. "We had one old laying hen that nested up near the fence corner, and it was generally her nest what got picked. Paw put the trap under it and locked up the hen so's she wouldn't spring it herself. Couple days later, it got tripped. And happened I was the first one out'n the house that morning. I found him.

"He was the youngest of the Meldrin brood, not more'n eight, maybe nine at the most. Just a scrawny little kid with a wild look to his face, like some kind of animal. He'd done himself bad by reaching through the fence to get at the eggs. It put him so'd he didn't stand a chance of getting that trap open. He was trying though, working like hell to fight them steel jaws open and tearing up his caught hand doing it. He'd got himself all over spattered with his own blood."

He jerked the tobacco pouch out of his pocket and began building another cigarette. "I come up on him and he looked at me. I swear to God I never seen nothing like the way he looked at me. He never hollered nor whimpered nor begged nor said anything at all. He just looked at me.

"Nora, there wasn't nothing else I *could* do. I opened up the trap. And he took off, never saying a thing. He just give a quick look over his shoulder like he thought

29

I'd chase him and tore off into the woods."

When he didn't say anything else, she asked him, "You got to know him after that?"

"No, none of the respectable folk around Jackson County ever got to know any of the Meldrins. I used to see him sometimes in the woods or in town, but he never said a word to me. Never even seemed like he knew me. I was off to the Army for a while and when I got back I'd run into him the same way. He'd growed and he'd got himself a revolver that I don't think he was ever without, but he didn't seem to have changed any other way. He'd look through me like he never even seen me.

"Sometimes I figured maybe he wasn't right in the head, but Mr. Grennell, who run the store, he said Clant could figure better'n his brothers and could read labels and the like, so I reckon it was just his way toward me. Maybe he figured it was me set the trap in the first place."

"Lamar," Nora interrupted, "you can't hold yourself responsible for something your father did. It wasn't you who set that wolf trap. You're not responsible to Meldrin for that."

"No, I didn't set it." He shook his head slowly. "But it was me let him out of it. If I hadn't, Paw would have got him and seen he got sent off to some proper institution and taught decent ways. Only *I* let him out.

"Nora, that wasn't no way for a young 'un to be growing up. The Meldrins were a purely bad bunch. They raided for horses and whatever else they could loot, and sometimes it seemed like they done it just for the hell of burning down houses and seeing folks made miserable. Young as he was, Clant was riding right along with the rest of 'em.

30

"I recall when old man Pike, who never done nobody no harm and didn't hardly own enough to make him worth robbing, made it into town with a ball in his shoulder. They'd rode in masked and run off what stock he had and put his place to the torch, crops and all. He said that the one that put the ball in him wasn't but a kid—a boy that used his gun left-handed. He said if they ever got took, he could stand up in court and identify the boy on account he'd seen the scars on the young 'un's right wrist."

"Clant Meldrin?"

"They never proved it on him. Pike's wound putrefied and he died of it. Fact is, nobody ever got close enough to any of the Meldrins to jail 'em. Not then. A couple of the boys got killed but none never got caught. Not until a lot later." Glynn got to his feet again and walked to the door. He looked out at the lead-gray sky. "Won't be long till it snows," he said as he turned back toward Nora.

He still had more to say, she thought. There were more things he had to get out of his mind and into the open. She asked, "What about the Meldrins?"

"Come the peace they kept right on riding the way they had been. Then they got some other boys in with them and took to robbing stages and banks and the like. Got real ambitious.

"I guess they done well enough for a while. It must have been close onto four years after the war when they tried for the bank at Bloomington. Only one of the boys they'd took in with them—one that wasn't their kind—he sold them out. When they rode into Bloomington, they rode into a trap."

"What happened?"

"Mostly they got killed off making a stand in the

31

streets. But Clant and his brother, Isham, and one of the other boys lived through getting shot down and they come to trial. Considering what people knew against them, they got off right easy. Folks figured they should all have been hanged, but the law's a funny thing sometimes. Only thing they actually got tried for was that one attempted bank robbery, and then it couldn't be proved any one of them had actually killed nobody. The judge was a reconstructionist who listened to what they claimed about the hard time they'd had on account of the war. He let Isham off with a seven-year sentence.

"And Clant, he wasn't even full-growed then, sixteen, maybe seventeen at most—well, the judge gave him a good hard talking-to and sentenced him to three years. The rest of his time he made for himself."

She looked at him questioningly, and he explained, "Clant didn't take too good to prison. He raised so much hell they added on to his time. When he'd finished out the three years that the judge had sentenced him to, he found himself with another year to serve for troublemaking. That was when he stopped fighting them. Real sudden, he settled like a bucked-out bronc and finished his time just as peaceable as you could ask. That's what give me the notion maybe he could still be broke to pull to harness, if he'd put his mind to it. What trouble he's got into since he was released is all small stuff, drinking and fist-fighting and the like. He's shied real clear of anything that might put him back into prison. I reckon that's a start."

"You've kept track of him all this time?" she asked.

He shrugged. "It wasn't hard. I've got friends all over the country, from the days back when I was with Wells Fargo, and I know a lot of lawmen around who've kept an eye on him for me. I kept hoping our trails would

32

cross sometime. I got a strong notion that if he was handled proper he'd gentle down."

"You feel it's your responsibility to gentle him?"

"It was me turned him loose," he said. "Nora, fact is, I'm afraid in time he'll forget how much he's scared of getting sent back to prison. He'll only remember all the jobs he's been fired off and all the times he's gone hungry. If he ain't been broke to harness by then—if he goes back to the Meldrin ways—I reckon it'll be my responsibility to kill him."

CHAPTER 4

IT WAS MIDMORNING OF THE SECOND DAY WHEN Clant Meldrin came into the Stove Rocks. He'd camped in their shadow on the slopes of Bloodyhead Mountain and had risen late, after lying wrapped in his saddle blanket until the sun had gotten high enough to take the mists up off the meadows and to put a little of its warmth into the air. Then he'd ridden a direct trail into the rocks.

He followed a game path, with Dog casting ahead reading scents and taking joy in the brisk new day. But as the trail narrowed and twisted into the rocks, he called the dog back to trot along near the horse. And when he came to the overhang of the cliffs, he drew rein and whistled.

The whistle was returned and a shadow moved in the rocks ahead and above. A man, rifle in hand, appeared on a crest of rock and waved.

Clant waved back and rode on in, both hands on the reins now, held high and well clear of the saddle. He moved the dun along at an easy walk, turning right and

33

then left and up, going through the rocks and into the little canyon.

It was a small basin, about the size of a horse corral, walled by upthrusts of rock and the overhanging face of a cliff. Within the clearing there were a couple of Osnaburgs roped over poles to make lean-tos, and not far from the cliff face a makeshift tripod held a black iron kettle over the glowing embers of a fire. There was a big smoke-stained coffeepot sitting in the ashes and as he rode in, Clant sniffed the inviting scent of the coffee.

The dark-haired girl working at the wreck box glanced up and smiled at him. He grinned and waved at her; then he looked around at the men who lounged in the clearing. They'd seen him ride in and they'd known before that that he was on the trail. But they paid him no particular attention.

As he drew rein a man stepped out of one of the lean-tos and ambled toward him. He was broad-built and sandy-haired, with a full mustache and an unkempt scruff of whiskers on his jaw. He had on a jacket, but no shirt. The front of his faded red flannels showed between the lapels of the coat.

"Mornin', Clant," he said as he halted and tucked his thumbs under his galluses. With a hospitable grin that wasn't reflected in his pale blue eyes, he added, "Step down and have a plate of frijoles."

Clant swung a leg over the cantle and dropped off the horse. "Mornin', Paul," he muttered as he headed toward the fire. He accepted the tin dish the dark-headed girl held out and scooped himself a bait of spiced beans from the kettle. Giving the girl another grin, he turned back to Paul Fairweather and asked, "How've things been up here?"

"Nice and quiet, Clant. You pick up anything
34

interesting in town?"

He nodded as he fingered the deputy's badge out of his pocket. He held it up, flashing sunlight on it.

"Where'd you get that?" Fairweather asked suspiciously. "You didn't kill yourself no lawman, did you?"

"No. Got me a new job."

"*Cómo*?"

"The sheriff down to Jubilee give it to me," Clant told him. "I kinda got fired from off that riding job for Tatum, so Sheriff Glynn up and asked me to work for him. Dollar a day and found."

Fairweather studied him a moment; then he chuckled. "Damn me, boy, sometimes you do beat all. You really mean it, don't you?"

Clant turned the star in his hands as he looked at it and mumbled, "I ain't reckon they was ever a *Meldrin* who was a lawman before."

"Ain't likely," Fairweather agreed. "How the hell *you* come onto it?"

"This Sheriff Glynn give me my choice of the job or jail. I ain't much care for his jail so I took the job." He shoved the badge back into his pocket.

Fairweather chuckled again and shook his head. Then he asked, "What about that money? You find out about it for me?"

"Couldn't get nothing about what train it'd be on, but I heard Stacy from the bank telling old man Tatum how he expected to have it in his safe on the first of the month."

Pursing his lips, Fairweather nodded. "I'd sooner take it out the bank than off the train anyways."

"First of the month," Clant said again. He glanced toward the sky. "Gonna be right cold up here by then.

Likely come snow before long."

"Snow don't bother me none. It'll just make it that much harder traveling for any kind of a posse they try to set after me."

"That Sheriff Glynn is a right determined type of man, Paul. He ain't gonna let a little snow turn him off your trail."

Fairweather's eyes narrowed. "What's the matter with you, Clant? You trying to tell me something?"

"Nothing. Only just the sheriff told me to give you a message if I was to run onto you. He said likely you'd do best to move yourself out'n here before it started in to snow."

Fairweather made a slight gesture with one hand and several of the men loafing around moved in closer. Clant glanced at them; then he looked back as Fairweather asked, "How's that sheriff know I'm here, *amigo*? How friendly did you and him get when he give you that badge?"

"You think I've took up with the law?"

"I think it's kinda peculiar for that sheriff to give *you* a badge, boy. What did you do in return for it?"

"If I'd took that badge for anything but laughs I'd have better sense than to come up here showing it around," Clant said. "Paul, that sheriff down to Jubilee is a feller from back to Missouri who done me a turn once. I reckon he figures I owe him for it. Now he figures I'll pay him back by crossing you."

"*Do* you owe him something, *amigo*?"

"Hell, I never asked him no favor. He's got no call to ask me none. And I ain't doing him none."

"Then how does he know I'm here in these hills?"

" 'Cause you and your boys ain't know no better'n to advertise yourselves. Some rannihan from the Jay-Bar

36

was popping beef out'n the brush up this way and he come onto your sign, the same way I done. He got a look at you, too, Paul. It was him that told the sheriff. What I got asked to do was ride up here and see if I could find out where you'd set, maybe get the lay of your outfit. Sheriff figured if you seen me you wouldn't suspicion me the way you would him."

Fairweather considered. He nodded and asked, "What you plan on telling that sheriff when you get back down there?"

"I ain't exactly planned I'd be seeing him again," Clant said, and then stuffed his mouth with beans.

"Why not?" Fairweather had to wait until Clant had finished swallowing to get an answer.

"Ain't nothing back there in Jubilee for me but trouble."

"There'll be a nice piece of hard money in that bank for you come the first of the month, Clant. You interested in that?"

"You ain't paid me yet for what I already done for you."

"You'll get paid after we've pulled off the job."

"Un-ugh," Clant grunted, and shook his head. "You made me a deal, Paul. Cash money for information. I've give you the information. Now you give me the cash money. *Sí, amigo?*"

With a smile, Fairweather said, "You've had a fair ride up here. Why don't you settle and rest yourself? Finish off the frijoles and have some coffee. We can palaver later."

"You palaver all you want. I ain't change my mind," Clant shrugged. He scooped another bait of beans off the plate as he drifted back toward the fire.

"Coffee, Angel?" he asked the dark-headed girl.

37

"*Sí, pronto,*" she answered, looking up at him. Her eyes were as dark as her hair and there was fire in their depths. She was damned pretty, in that special Mex way that came from Spanish and Indian blood. The thick woolen shirt she had on pretty much covered the fullness of her bosom, but the pair of men's britches stretched tight over the roundness of her rump and full thighs. Clant looked her over with admiration in his face as he seated himself on the ground. He leaned back against the rock of the cliff and watched Dog nose into the wreck box and get a slap in the face from Angel. Then the animal drifted over and settled himself at Clant's side. He finished off the beans and set the plate on the ground for the dog to lick.

The sunlight was warming and, with his belly full, Clant felt a strong temptation to let himself sleep. He closed his eyes; then he opened them at a sound from the lean-to.

The girl who pushed aside the Osnaburg flap and stepped out was a pale blonde; she was almost matchstick thin. When she saw him she waved and started toward him, gathering her full skirts and walking with a peculiar studied grace. She looked like a scrawny tow-headed little kid imitating the fancy manners of her elders. Her eyes, the blue of the columbine, were a child's eyes. It wasn't until she got close that he could see the marks of the years in the skin around her eyes and on her neck. Clant had wondered at times whether she might be some years older than he himself.

As she came up to him, he stirred and got to his feet. He pulled off his hat and swept it in front of him in the mockery of a bow. "Mornin', Lady."

With a pleased smile, she curtsied. "Mornin', Clant. It's nice to see you again." Her voice was high and thin, like that of a reed pipe. "Lord knows, you're right about the only *gentleman* ever comes callin' up here."

"You're nigh about the only lady ever calls me a gentleman." He grinned at her. "Set and have some coffee with me, ma'am." He slapped the hat back onto his head and offered her his hand as she smoothed her skirts and seated herself on the ground. Then he settled down next to her.

It was a game he'd learned at Fairweather's camp in Texas—putting on manners for Lady. Some of the men amused themselves by doing it now and then and it pleased her—the way having somebody throw sticks for him to fetch pleased Dog. But Dog seemed to understand that it was a game. Lady never did. She never seemed to see the mockery in the bows or to hear it in the voices.

"Some of them friends of Paul's got manners when they think about it," she was saying. "But mostly they don't never think about it. They ain't nothing but a bunch of swamp rats." She favored that name as the lowest insult she could give a man. But nobody who knew Lady ever got mad about her insults.

It amused Clant. "I reckon I'm kinda a swamp rat myself," he said. Looking toward the dark-headed girl, he called, "Angel, that coffee 'bout ready for drinking?"

"You want coffee, you fetch it yourself," she snapped back at him, shooting a dark glance at Lady.

"What ol' swamp you come from?" Lady asked curiously.

"Big'n down to Ware County in Georgia," he answered. "You and Angel have a fallin' out?"

"Her! She ain't got no manners nohow," Lady said. She turned up her nose and sniffed with what she took to be genteel dignity. "*I'll* fetch us coffee, Clant." She scrambled to her feet and in a moment was back with two tins brim-full of the thick black Rio. As she handed him a cup and settled beside him again, she asked, "Georgia swamp anything like a Carolina swamp?"

"I ain't know. I ain't remember Georgia swamps none too good. We got run out before I was nigh big enough for 'gator bait," he told her. "And I ain't never seen a Carolina swamp."

"They ain't much to look at. Just ol' black water and trees and bugs and shanty-houses up on poles."

"That sounds about like what I recollect," he muttered.

"It ain't nothing to the big house *I* come from. That were a thing to see, Clant. Big or red brick house with these thick white things what they call columns up the front of it, and more glass winders than you ever seen . . ."

He sipped the coffee and leaned his head back against the rock as she began to describe the big house again. It was the thing she seemed to enjoy the most—talking about that place. And the description was always the same.

It must have been a real house, he figured, and she must have spent a mess of time looking at it to be able to recall so many things about it. She seemed to know every brick, every window pane, and every bush in the hedge—from the outside. But if you asked her about the inside, the way the fellers sometimes did to tease, her descriptions got vague and changed from telling to telling. Only the big chandelier stayed the same. And you could see it through the front windows.

He listened to the thin singsong of her voice as if it were a melody, not hearing the words that he'd already heard at least half a dozen times during the few week he'd camped with Fairweather in Texas, and again the last time he'd called here in Stove Rocks. But it didn't bother him any to listen again.

He worked his fingers into the scruff hair of Dog's neck and relaxed under the warm sun. It was pleasant to sit with Lady, pleasant to be aware of the happiness she got from having someone listen to her talk.

That was a funny thing about people, he thought as he listened. The way talking could be so damned important to them. There might be an odd man here or there who could get along fine without he ever spoke a word or heard so much as a "Good morning" from another man, but such as those were far between, he'd decided. Most of the loners and the hermits held come onto were at least a little crazy.

As far back as he could remember, he'd known that sometimes a man has to be alone. He has to get the hell away from other people and their talking before it addles his wits. It wasn't until he'd been sent off to the penitentiary that he'd learned it worked the other way around, too. It was the first time in his life he'd ever been *that* alone. Locked in a damned black hole with no sound but what he made himself, no light, and hardly enough air to breathe, he'd reached the opinion that there were times when just the sound of another voice, just the chance to speak a word and know someone heard it, could get to be more important to a man than food or water.

Afterwards, he'd watched and studied people and he'd come to the conclusion that other men had the same feelings. It was a strange thing, the need a man had for other people. And a strong thing—like a chain on him, keeping him from being his own master.

"Clant!"

41

He opened his eyes and looked at Lady.

"You done went and fell off asleep, didn't you?" she scolded. "A real gentleman don't fall asleep when a lady's talking at him."

He grinned at her guiltily and rubbed his knuckles over the reddish stubble on his jaw.

"That's another thing," she said. "A *gentleman* don't come calling on a lady without he's shaved nor washed his face off, neither."

"Texas Paul always shave afore he calls on you?" he asked.

She looked away and admitted, "Paul ain't hardly always a gentleman. Nowadays he ain't hardly never one. Not since he took on that Angel woman."

"You and Angel ain't get on too good together?"

"She's *fat!* That's why Paul likes her, on account she's so fat. Like an ol' cow."

Clant glanced around. Angel had finished up at the wreck box and was working away at something else across the clearing. She bent over as he watched and he thought to himself that if she was fat, it was damn sure just the right amount and in just the right places.

"Ain't no lady get herself fat like that," Lady was saying. "But she ain't nothin', just a dirty ol' *pelado*. Ain't nobody takes his hat off to her." She eyed Clant and added, "Ain't none of these swamp rats would scrape his whiskers just to go calling on her."

He scrubbed his hand over his jaw again. It was an easy enough thing Lady was asking of him—just that he put on a show of favoring her and respecting her whims. She'd been Paul's regular woman for a long time; the airs she'd put on and the notion she held that she was quality had amused him enough that he'd played along at the game. Now it looked like Paul had taken a fancy

42

to the full-bodied Mex girl and likely that cut real deep into Lady's pride. She needed for a man to show her some favors and treat her in the way she figured a real gentlewoman ought to be treated. It wouldn't be that much trouble, he decided, and it would please her.

He got to his feet and went to dig the razor out of his war bag. Likely it would please her considerable, he told himself, if he were to shave and clean up and come back with a handful of them kinnikinnick leaves and berries made up into a regular bouquet. As he stripped off his shirt he was thinking he might stay the night— and if Paul did favor the Mex girl now, well, Texas Paul was an uncommon generous man when there was no money involved. He wasn't at all given to being greedy about his women.

He'd seen Paul ride off with a couple of the boys and he hoped they'd gone meat-hunting. Maybe they'd bring back a deer. He'd had plenty-enough of eating Texas venison back at Tatum's ranch. That Box T coosie could make even good beef taste like it'd been cut out of an old saddle skirt.

He'd finished shaving and was bent over the bucket splashing water in his face when he heard the laugh. Wiping his eyes, he looked over his shoulder at Angel. She'd come up close behind him and was standing hipshot, smiling at him.

"*Cómo*?" he asked. "What's funny?"

"Funny?" She pursed her lips and pouted slightly. Reaching out, she touched a finger to his bare shoulder and looked critically at his back. When she spoke again, it wasn't an answer to his question. She edged her voice with that sympathetic concern a woman puts on when she's after making a man fancy her. "You have convict stripes on your back."

"I know," he said.

"Why did they whip you?" She ran her finger along the edge of his shoulder blade and across a welted scar.

"For making trouble."

"Did you make much trouble?"

He grinned. "I reckon so. For most of my time."

"A man hit me with a whip once," she said, tracing her finger along the welt.

"Bullwhip?" he asked with interest.

She shook her head. "Quirt."

"Where'd he hit you?"

She put her hand on her rump and grinned at him. "Guadalajara. He was *muy hombre.*" She looked as if she was enjoying the recollection. Laughing, she poked him in the ribs.

He swung his arm, catching her up and pulling her close against his bare chest. She squirmed against him, making as if she meant to get loose, and he tightened his grip on her. Even through the thickness of the wool shirt she wore, he could feel the beating of her heart. Or maybe it was his own that he felt. He caught her mouth with his.

She returned the kiss fiercely, struggling at the same time. Her teeth sank into his lip, nibbling at it the way Dog would sometimes worry at his hand. Then suddenly she clamped down hard.

He bit her back and released her mouth. He could taste salt on his tongue and wondered if she'd brought blood.

"*Muy hombre,*" she said in it voice that was all breath. Rising on her toes, she grabbed at his mouth with hers. With her lips, her teeth, her tongue— viciously—she kissed him. Her arms were around his neck, her nails clawing into his bare back.

44

"Clant."

The voice was Fairweather's. *Damn him,* Clant thought as he shoved the girl away and looked up.

The outlaw sat on a horse that was snorting and lathered under the rein. He'd come back fast. But he didn't look worried. With a smirking grin he leaned on the pommel and asked, *"Muy hombre?"*

"Muy muchacha," Clant answered. *"Qué pasa?"*

"We got company, *amigo.*" Fairweather gave a jerk of his head toward the entrance of the clearing.

Clant wheeled and saw the horsemen coming through the gap in the rocks. They were Fairweather's men, the two who'd ridden out with him. And there was a stranger with them.

A stranger? Clant stared at the third man as he drew rein and stepped down off his mount. His blue wool shirt was stiff, with the store creases still showing in it, and the broad-brimmed hat that shadowed his face looked as if it hadn't yet been rained on.

He was a big man, taller and broader than Clant, but with the same kind of long-boned frame. And the ragged stubble of whiskers on his face were of the same dirty claybank color as Clant's.

He shoved back the hat and squinted against the sunlight as he stepped forward. Looking into his face, Clant felt as if he were looking into a mirror that showed him back himself in another ten years.

"'My God," he mumbled. "Isham!"

CHAPTER 5

WITH THE SMIRKING GRIN STILL ON HIS FACE, Fairweather said, "I figured you two would be right surprised to run onto each other."

Clant nodded slightly as he stared at his brother. "Damned surprised," he thought to himself.

It was Isham who made the move. He turned the corners of his mouth into a smile of sorts and said heartily, "Right! Clant, boy, it's good to see you again." He took a step forward and held out a big work-hard hand.

Even as Isham's fingers wrapped around his, Clant knew what was going to happen. Ish clamped down, pressuring the knuckles together and, right-handed, Clant didn't have the strength to fight back. Setting his teeth, he clenched his left hand to slam it into his brother's gut. But suddenly Isham let go.

Clant held rein on his temper. Turning deliberately, he picked up his shirt and shrugged it on, as Isham asked, "You changed any, all these years, boy?"

"I can still handle a gun, if that's what you mean," he answered. "You?"

Isham grinned.

"It ain't seven years yet," Clant said. "You hang out your wash?"

"No," Isham's grin broadened with pride, "I've been released, free and clear. A man behaves himself, they give him time off his sentence. *I* ain't such a damn fool as to serve no longer'n I had to."

That cut deep, just as Isham had meant it to. It hurt worse than the handshake. Clant turned his attention to working the plug out of his pocket and biting off a chunk. Coming onto Isham here this way—it had been too sudden. He had to think it out. He had to hang onto his temper until he'd had a chance to go over his thoughts.

"They banked your fire a mite, ain't they, boy?" Ish said. With a self-satisfied smile, he clapped a hand on Clant's shoulder. "Ne'mind. You in with Paul and me?"

Clant pulled out from under the hand. "No, I'm cutting my own trail nowadays."

"Oh?" Isham said, as if he didn't believe it.

"Come on, have some coffee, Ish," Paul called from the fire. He picked up the pot and filled two cups.

Isham slapped his hand down on Clant's shoulder again, pressuring him to turn. "Come on, boy, let's us set and talk. It's been a long time, ain't it?"

Fairweather handed a cup to Isham and said, "I'm sure as hell glad you could make it in time, *amigo*. This is gonna be a right nice little job."

"I'm real happy I could make it myself," Isham agreed. He had a deep, rough voice that had a good-natured sound, as if he were always about to start laughing. It didn't fit in with the look of his eyes at all.

Clant tilted himself a cup of the Rio and followed them into the lean-to. Once they'd settled, Fairweather began outlining his plans to upend the Jubilee bank and shake out the shipment of hard money that would be there on the first of the month. He finished off by telling Isham about the deputy's star Clant had brought in with him.

Isham pounded his knee as he leaned back his head and laughed with a roar like a bull. "Dam'est thing I ever heard," he said when he had caught his breath. "That's right clever for you, Clant. What name you been

47

using down to town?"

"My own," Clant muttered.

Isham looked surprised. "Who is this damn fool sheriff what hired you on?"

"Name of Lamar Glynn. Maybe you recall him, Ish. He come from back to Jackson County."

"Yeah, I recall him. A psalm-singer. Don't recall as how you and him was friends, though."

"Friends?" Clant said, as if it were a word he didn't know.

Isham turned to Fairweather again. "Paul, what say we send the boy here back down to Jubilee? He can keep a close watch on this sheriff from inside the law office if he plays along with this deputy job. Anything changes down there or the sheriff gets more suspicious or the like, the boy here can get us word of it. And come the job, the boy'll be in just the place to put a couple bullets in ol' Glynn's back. Ain't that so, boy?"

Clant made no answer.

"Right!" Fairweather said heartily.

Isham emptied his coffee cup and held it out, "Fetch me some more, boy."

Clant got slowly to his feet. His urge to shove a boot into Isham's face and walk out was strong. But he didn't do it. Instead he took the cup and headed for the fire.

He hunkered down, holding the cup in his right hand as he tilted the pot over it. It slipped suddenly, sliding through his fingers and splashing the steaming coffee on the ground.

"Goddammit," he muttered through his teeth. He gave the cup a hard name and put his hand to it again. But his fingers wouldn't close around it. He hated them—Isham, Fairweather, Glynn, everyone else—he hated them all.

48

"*Amigo*?" It was Angel. She looked down at him curiously and asked, "What's the matter?"

"Nothing!" he snapped at her.

She started to say something more, and then shrugged. With a glance toward the lean-to, she asked, "The big one, he is your brother?"

"Yeah."

She nodded to herself. "He is *muy hombre*?"

"Likely he is," Clant muttered in reply.

Picking up the cup, Angel held it under the spout of the coffeepot. When he made no move to fill it, she pushed his hand off the pot and upended it herself. Then she held the cup toward him.

"It's for Isham," he said, jerking his head toward the lean-to.

Smiling to herself, the girl rose and ducked under the Osnaburg flap with the cup.

Clant waited, expecting to hear Ish hollering for him to return. Well, let him holler, he told himself, and see what it gets him. But he had a sick feeling that when Isham called, he'd answer.

"Clant?"

It wasn't Isham who had called. The voice was Lady's. He got to his feet and looked for her.

She'd climbed up into the rocks a way and was sitting there in the warmth of the sun with her skirts spread around her. He looked at her thinking how stubbornly she insisted on always wearing those full skirts. Even when Fairweather and his men were riding hard, even though she had to ride astride to stay with them, she refused to change into britches the way Angel did. The skirts would billow up, showing her knees in a way that would have horrified real quality folk. But she maintained that a *lady* would never put on men's clothes

49

and she held fast against all the urging that she do different.

Clant wondered what it would be like to be so strong in your mind about something that nobody could force you to do different.

When he looked at her, she smiled and called, "Come on up and set with me, Clant."

It seemed like a good idea. A damn good idea. He scrambled up the rocks and settled himself next to her in the sunlight.

"What are you doing up here?" he asked.

"I kinda wanted to be alone."

"Then what'd you call me up here for?"

She plucked a grass stalk from a crack in the rocks and slit it with her thumbnail. "Ain't much fun being alone all by yourself."

He pulled up a blade of the grass and blew against it. Lady smiled at the whistle it made and asked him, "Can you make a tune that way?"

"Not as I know of," he answered. "Best way to make a tune is on a banjo."

"Banjo is the devil's instrument," she said sternly.

"I always heard his instrument was the fiddle."

She nodded. "I've heard that, but it ain't so."

"How you know?"

"Back to the big house where I lived, we had fancy parties all the time and we had fiddlers to them. We wouldn't of had no fiddles if they was bad. You should have seen them parties, Clant. Us ladies all done ourselves up in nigh the prettiest clothes you ever seen and come to the door in carriages, and the darkies held the horses while our gentlemen friends helped us down off'n the carriages, and when the door opened up for us to go in, the music all come rushing out at us and it

50

would plumb shiver up your backbone to hear it," She began to hum a piece of a tune.

"Sing me something, Lady," he said. He leaned back with his hands under his head. The sun was bright on his eyelids, and he covered his face with his hat.

" 'What blood's that on your shirt front, Son Davy, Son Davy, What blood's that on your shirt front, the truth come tell to me . . . ,' " she began. Her voice was thin and very small, especially there in the open, but it was as true as a church bell. And it was as sad as the bell when it calls folks to a burial.

By the time she came to the end of the song, Clant had propped himself up on his elbow and was watching her as he listened to the words. When she stopped singing, he asked, "That feller, Davy, he up and killed his own brother?"

She nodded.

"I ain't understand it," he said. "How come he'd kill his own blood brother over him cutting down some old willow tree?"

"I don't know. The song don't say."

"It ain't make no sense," he muttered. "Was it some special kind of willow tree?"

"Song don't say," she repeated. "There's a mess of them willow trees in the old songs. They're always in the sad songs."

"You know any songs what ain't sad?"

"I reckon," she admitted. "But all the songs about fancy folk—about kings and queens and lords and ladies and such—they're all sad. All about people dying and getting killed and getting hanged and the like."

Clant nodded, recollecting the songs he knew. "Them fancy folk, they kill a man, they get hanged same as the rest of us, ain't they?"

51

"Songs say they do," she answered. "Only sometimes they buy out'n it with money." She started into another song: " 'Hangman, hangman, slack up your rope . . .' "

He interrupted her. "You don't sing me no hanging song, Lady. They make my neck itch."

"Is somebody looking to hang you, Clant?" she asked.

"Aint right now," he answered her. "But if that brother of mine gets his way, likely they will be."

"Why?"

"He's got a notion for me to kill that sheriff down to Jubilee."

"You gonna do it?"

He scrubbed at the gravel on the rock with his fingertip. "Likely," he said.

"But you don't want to do it?"

"No."

She looked at him. She had a feeling he meant to say more, so she waited.

After a moment he spoke again. "That's the way it's always been. When I was a young 'un, it was Pap with his 'Fetch me some eggs for breakfast, boy,' or Bob with his 'Unsaddle my horse, boy,' or Isham hollering, 'Fetch me the jug out in the crick, boy.' Hell, I ain't hardly knowed I had more name than 'boy' till I was half-growed. Then it come to be one or another of 'em hollering, 'Clant, you fire that haystack,' or 'Clant, run them horses on down the road,' or 'Clant, put a pistol ball in that old man.' " He paused again and she waited, knowing from the tone of his voice that he wasn't finished yet with what he had to say.

He gazed down at the gravel under his finger as he said, "After them it was the goddamn penitentiary. You think Pap and the boys was bad, you ain't know

52

nothing. Worst Pap ever done was beat the hell out'n me. But them fellers—Lady, I'd sooner get hanged than go back there."

"I've seen a mess of hangings," she told him. "When they hanged my pa, it weren't so bad on account they used a reg'lar derrick and done it right. But last year when the posse strung up Johnny Scarver off a cottonwood, he was awful hard dying."

"They use a lariat?"

She nodded.

"It ain't no good to hang a man with a lariat. The rope ain't thick enough. You got to have a rope you can put a real proper heavy knot in and you got to set it right to his jaw, else it don't break his neck when he falls."

"That so?" she asked curiously.

"Sure," he said. "You got to drop him right, too. A posse ain't generally know nothing about dropping a man. They use a rope whats got stretch in it, or ain't slack enough, all they do is strangle him. That's slow, hard dying. That's how come sometimes a posse'll put a few bullets in a man, once he's on the rope. If they done it the right way, though, his neck'd snap and he'd die decent-quick."

"Some of them posses don't want a man to die too quick," she said thoughtfully. "Some of them like to watch him die real hard and slow."

"Yeah," he agreed.

"Why you reckon that is?"

"Likely just plain meanness. They's a mess of people in this world take their pleasure from just plain meanness. The more miserable they make a person, the more pleasure they get out'n it."

"That don't seem right."

"It's the way it is, though."

She nodded but made no answer, and after a moment he said, "Hanging's a skill, like throwing a gun. There can't just anybody up and do it right. Even off a gallows it ain't always done right. When I was in the penitentiary, I heard about some feller what they give too much rope for the weight of him. He dropped hard and it pulled the head right off him."

"You reckon it hurt?"

"Likely." He thought it over. "Better'n strangling though, I reckon. Damn sight quicker. I hear tell this new feller they got to Fort Smith is a real good hangman. 'Bout the best they is. German feller. I hear they hang near everybody down to Fort Smith now."

"I don't care how good they is," Lady decided, "I don't think I'd like much to get hanged."

"It ain't hardly ever they hang wimmen. It ain't proper. Even a posse will hardly ever put a rope on a woman."

She looked at him. "I don't think I'd much like it if you was to get hanged, either."

"Hell, it ain't nothing I got my mind set on doing. How come us to get to talking on this way anyhow?"

She thought a moment. "On account your brother wants you to kill that ol' sheriff down to Jubilee."

"Yeah," he muttered, sorry that she'd recalled the thought to him.

"Why don't you just tell him *no*?" she asked. "Tell him you ain't gonna do it."

"Used to be I'd tell them that," he said. "Used to be I'd buck up to Pap and he'd lay the strap onto me. Else I'd sass back one of my brothers and get my teeth rattled. I took me some damn fine licking afore I'd give in. Didn't do me much good though. Always end up the same way. Always come to it, I'd give in and do what I

54

was told. I reckon I will this time, too."

"You gonna fight your brother before you do what he tells you?"

"Maybe. I ain't know for sure till the time comes," he answered. "In prison they got a notion of breaking a man out of the habit of saying *no* to what he's told. Only once I got out, I figured I wasn't gonna let myself get into no more spots where I was gonna be ordered around that way."

"I can't watch if you're gonna fight him," she said. "It ain't proper for a lady to watch men fighting."

"No?"

She shook her head. "Is fighting fun?" she asked.

"Not always. Sometimes I get a gizzardful with all the time doing it. Sometimes I figure I'm gonna quit and not fight with nobody who don't start it first. I ain't done it yet though."

She studied a moment. "You ought to quit. A feller what's as much a gentleman as you are ought not all the time be hitting people sudden when they ain't expecting it. It ain't mannerly."

"You reckon it's mannerly to go around shooting sheriffs in the back?"

"Sheriffs ain't no proper gentlemen."

"This one is," he said. "He's worse'n a preacher. He's the kind of damn fool what'll got out'n his way to be fair with a man. Take himself a strong chance of getting into trouble doing it. Folks in the county ain't likely gonna admire the way he's been messing around with me."

"Why'd he do it, then?"

"Hell, I ain't know."

"You like him?" she asked.

It was a strange question. And when he considered it,

the answer was strange too. He admitted, "I reckon I could if I set my mind to it."

She plucked another grass stem and twisted it around her fingers. "You like Angel, too?"

"I reckon so." He looked at her curiously, wondering what she meant by that.

"Angel likes you," she said. "Angel likes everybody except me. Leastways she likes all the menfolk. A man up and treats me nice and right away she goes sniffing around, making up to him like she was some ol' she-hound. I seen her."

So that was it. He asked, "You mad at me for kissing her?"

She gave a shake of her head. "Everybody kisses Angel. Ol' she-hound. I don't want to talk about her no more!" She looked at the grass stem and added softy, "Except only—only—Clant, you think *she'd* care if you was to up and get yourself hanged?"

"No, I ain't reckon she would," he owned.

Lady smiled to herself. Plucking at another grass stem, she began to hum to herself and in a moment started singing the words: " 'Little birdie, little birdie, come and sing me your song. I've a short time to be here with you and a long time to be gone . . . . . ' "

"Clant!"

He started as if the call had been the shake of a snakes rattles. Squinting, he looked down toward the lean-to. Isham was standing there by the flap, his feet apart and his hands on his hips. He was staring up at them.

"Boy, you fetch yourself on down. You hear?" he shouted.

As Clant started down the rock, Lady called to him, "I can't watch if you're gonna fight."

56

"I ain't gonna fight," he answered her, with an edge of disgust in his voice.

"Come on here," Isham said as he reached the ground. "Paul and me got our plans all figured. We got us a good part in this for you, boy. Give you an even share in the take. We gotta get you headed back to Jubilee."

"I ain't figured on leaving till morning," Clant said.

Isham looked up at the sky. "You leave quick, you'll be there before tomorrow night."

"And I ain't figured on going back to Jubilee."

"You hear me, boy?" Ish said. When Clant didn't answer, he repeated it, "You hear me, boy?"

"Yeah, Ish. I hear you."

"Now, boy, what we want you to do is just go back down to that town and stay real close to that sheriff. If anything changes or looks to give us trouble, you get word back to me. If nothing looks to go wrong, we'll be riding in midafternoon on the first. When the shooting starts, all you have to do is take care of that sheriff and anybody else you get a bead on. But you gotta be sure the sheriff is too dead to lead any posse after us himself. You hear?"

Clant nodded.

"That's all you got to do. You can handle that can't you, boy?"

"Yeah."

" 'Tween now and then, you just behave yourself and get as friendly with that fool sheriff as you can. You understand, boy?"

"Yeah."

"All right, fetch on your horse and head back down."

Clant collected the dun and whistled Dog up from his rabbit-hunting. As he swung into the saddle, he said to

Isham, "Gimme some hard money, Brother."

"What for?"

"Spendin'."

"Hell, you got a job, boy. Go collect your dollar a day off'n that sheriff." Isham laughed and gave the dun a hard slap on the rump. He watched as Clant rode off, with the dog trotting along behind him. As Fairweather came up to his side, he muttered, "I'm gonna have to get rid of that hound of his."

"Why?" Fairweather asked.

Isham just grinned.

"He's a strange 'un," Fairweather said. "I didn't think he'd take the like of that off nobody. I mean the way you was telling him around."

Ish nodded in agreement. "Used to be he was a real short-fused young 'un. Sassed Pap all the time. Used to be I'd of had to knock him around a bit afore he'd of took that off me. Good thing, though, if he's learnt a little respect for his blood elders." He frowned thoughtfully. "You reckon maybe the penitentiary took the spine out'n him?"

Fairweather shrugged. "I've seen it happen to better men than him. But before you come, he stood up for himself often enough."

"Maybe nobody pushed him hard enough," Isham speculated. "Maybe he figured wouldn't none of you back him down the way he knows I will."

"Maybe," Fairweather agreed.

As they walked across the opening together, Isham asked, "You reckon he'll be any use to us?"

"He's got two things we can use him for. He's got a good gun hand and he's got that deputy's star."

"That's damn well all he's got," Isham muttered. "He ain't no good for nothing else."

CHAPTER 6

THE RAIN STARTED UP AGAIN A WHILE BEFORE SUNRISE. It didn't come down hard, but it kept on in a thin drizzle straight through the day, making traveling slow and very uncomfortable. It was still coming down when Clant reached Jubilee, well after dark.

He dropped rein in front of the sheriff's office and peeled his slicker as he stepped down off the dun horse. Throwing the slicker over the saddle, he ducked into the doorway of the office.

A lean, curly-headed young man, wearing a tin star on the front of a clean white shirt, sat in Sheriff Glynn's swivel chair with his heels on the desk. As he looked up at Clant his eyes clouded. Rubbing the still-sore bruise on his jaw, he asked sharply, "What do you want?"

Clant remembered Johnny Ward well enough. He remembered the way the deputy had accused him of stealing the dun horse and had gotten handcuffs on him when he'd tried to make a fight of it. He felt a dislike of Ward; it went deeper than that, though, and he didn't understand it any more than he understood the vague resentment he felt about the way Ward made himself at home behind Glynn's desk.

"Sheriff around?" he asked.

"He's gone for the day," Ward said. He swung his feet down off the desk and leaned forward, tense as a young bobcat.

The way Ward moved and the tone of his voice were like a challenge. Clant's hand eased into his pocket, his fingers wrapping around the stub of railroad spike. It might be real pleasant to smash a fist into that soft, scrubbed face and spill a little blood onto that neat white

59

shirt, he thought.

No, dammit! He let go the iron stub and moved his hand to a different pocket. Resting a shoulder against the doorframe, he fingered out the deputy's badge and flashed it. "Glynn tell you about this?"

Ward nodded. "He told me, all right. But I'll be damned if I can make sense of it."

"*You* ain't need to make sense of it." Clant shoved the star back into his pocket. He eyed the iron stove. From the doorway, he could feel the warmth of it; that damned miserable drizzle had managed to seep into the openings of his slicker and soak coldly into his bones. Moving indolently, he headed for it and rubbed his hands together in the waves of heat that rose from it.

Dog followed him into the room and began to shake the water out of his thick coat. He started to holler at the dog, but then he saw Ward jump as muddy droplets spattered on his shirt front.

"Get that damned animal out of here," Ward said, but Clant ignored him. Forcing the grin off his face, he turned and faced the deputy.

"Got any notion where Glynn might be?" he asked.

Ward looked as if he had a very good idea where the sheriff was. But he snapped back, "Why?"

"I done some riding for him," Clant said casually. "I reckoned he might want to see me."

"He'll be damned surprised to see you," Ward muttered.

"Why?"

"He figured you weren't coming back."

That didn't make much sense, Clant thought. If the sheriff had thought he'd leave for good, why had he gone through all that business about deputizing him? Why not just run him out of town? Glynn had damn

60

well acted like he *wanted* him to come back. Grinning slightly, he said to Ward, "I got lonesome for his jaw-wagging. Where you reckon I'll find him?"

"Around somewheres." Ward gave a shrug and lifted his feet back up onto the desk.

Without thinking, without planning it in any way, Clant swung. The blow was so sudden that it rocked Ward back out of the chair and sprawled him on the floor. He scrambled up and started to lunge. But he caught himself, balancing for an instant on the balls of his feet, and then stepped back.

Clant had the railroad spike in his hand again. Crouching slightly, he grinned to himself. It had been pleasant smashing a fist into the deputy's face. He wanted to do it again. But Ward had backed down. That seemed wrong. Why? He asked, "You aint want to fight?"

Ward shook his head sullenly. "Ain't much I'd ruther do. Only I gave Lamar my promise I'd lay off you, if you come back."

"Why?"

"I didn't reckon you would come back."

Clant shrugged and hooked his thumbs in his pants pockets. "You gonna tell me where to look for him, then?"

"You can damn well find him yourself," Ward muttered, as he settled himself back into the chair.

Looking at him, Clant got the feeling that hitting him again wouldn't get him any different an answer. And there wouldn't be much pleasure in it. There wasn't much pleasure in anything. Even the glow of the stove only warmed his skin. He stuffed his hand into his pocket and fingered the two-bit piece.

"Lend me a dollar," he said to Ward.

"Huh?"

"Give me lend of a dollar. This fire'll take the chill off a man's outside, but it don't warm him deep enough."

"What the hell makes you think I'd lend *you* money?"

"I'll pay it back. That sheriff owes me three days wage."

"Get it from him then."

That sounded like Isham, Clant thought darkly. You need something and ask somebody for it and all you get is kicked. Even by your own brother. Man's better off, he don't *ask*.

Clicking his tongue at the dog, he turned and headed for the door. Outside the rain had laid the dust of Long Street into a slick of mud. He slogged through it, head down against the rain, toward the Grand Pacific Palace saloon.

Two bits wouldn't buy enough liquor to warm the back of a man's tongue, he thought as he stepped up onto the plank walk. It sure wouldn't begin to take the edge of the chill he felt inside.

But as he pushed through the bat-wings another thought came to him. He paused and pinned the deputy's star on his vest before he walked up to the bar.

The bartender was a sociable sort, a full-mustached man called Tucker, who'd stand and talk with anybody. He eyed Clant curiously as he stepped up.

"Whiskey," Clant said, "And leave the bottle."

"You got the money?" Tucker asked, making the question firm and yet friendly at the same time.

"I ain't need the money," Clant answered, gesturing toward the star on his vest.

"You're in the wrong town, friend. A lawman in Jubilee pays for what he takes, same as any other citizen."

Clant leaned both elbows on the bar. "That's a hell of a way to run a town. What's the good of wearing a badge if you ain't get nothing for it but wages?"

"I wouldn't know," Tucker answered. "I never wore one." He swabbed at the mahogany with his bar-cloth. "So you really come back, did you?"

"You knowed I was away?"

"Sure. Everybody does. You reckon, it didn't shake this town by the ears when word got around about Lamar hiring you on in his office?"

"He been bragging about it or apologizing for it?" Clant asked.

"Neither. But word gets around."

Clant dug his fingers into his pocket and came up with the two-bit piece. Dropping it on the bar, he said, "Gimme a drink, Tuck."

The bartender poured a shot and set it in front of him. Then he shoved back the coin. "On the house," he said. "It ain't for that badge, though. You just made me a nice piece of change."

"How's that?"

"I had a dollar bet you *would* come back. Eight to one."

"You figured I would?" Clant asked, surprised.

"No." Tucker shook his head. "But I just can't resist them sort of odds."

That made sense. Clant grinned and emptied the glass. "Profit like that ought to be worth more'n one shot," he said as he put it down.

"Ain't a profit if I let you drink it all up," Tucker grumbled, but he filled the glass again. Then he turned away as someone upbar called for him.

Clant downed the shot, pocketed his quarter, and

63

headed for the street. He cut around a corner and across a back yard. He found the kind of dry spot he was looking for under the wide eaves of a house, against a chimney that had some warmth. He could see no lights in the windows and he hoped that the people inside were settled and asleep for the night.

Drawing the almost-full bottle from under his arm, he sat down by the chimney to warm the chill in his belly. Tucker would know damn well where that quart had gone, he thought as he opened it. He'd probably raise hell with Glynn about it, too. And maybe Glynn would run him out of town—before Isham and Fairweather rode down from the rocks. The first drag he took on the bottle was a long one.

Dog lay his big head against his thigh and politely refused the drink he offered.

Sometime or other he remembered that he'd set out to go somewhere or other to look for someone or other. He wasn't sure who or why, but he felt like there'd been a reason, and he decided maybe he'd better get on with it. The decision made, he set about the job of standing up. That turned out to be harder than he'd expected and by the time he was on his feet, he'd forgotten why he'd gone to all that trouble.

He took a tentative step from under the eaves and the rain hit him. It was cold and wet and miserable, but that was just fine. It was damn well what he deserved. He clamped his eyes shut and turned his face up toward the rain.

He'd lost his hat and the water began to soak into his hair. It trickled down the back of his neck and under his shirt collar and right on down his spine. He shivered. Turning his face down again, he wiped his eyes with the back of his hand.

It was Lamar Glynn he'd set out to look for. He remembered that much and asked himself why. Then he recalled Ish. Brother Isham had ordered him to kill the sheriff. Brother Isham was forever ordering him to do some damn thing or another. To hell with Brother Isham.

He walked on through the rain. It wasn't easy, not with the mud grabbing at his boots and sliding under his feet, threatening to throw him like a slippery bronc at every step. But damned if held let it. Damned if he'd let himself be thrown. Not when Brother Isham was waiting to pig him and crop his ears like he was some fool maverick. He had no intention of being branded like some damn piece of property.

They'd owned him for too damn long already. First Pap and his brothers. And then the damn state—like a horse or a beef—ordering him and driving him and tethering him and caging him. Too damn long. But he was his own man now . . .

He felt the ground twist out from under his feet and suddenly his face was in the mud-wet, slimy mud that stank of horses. He tried to prop himself up on his arms. He could hear somebody hollering. Whoever it was called out for Ish. But Ish was *his* brother. And then he knew that it was *him* hollering: "Ish, help me!"

But Ish wasn't there. Nobody was there. He was alone. Whatever had to be done, he had to figure it out for himself. Nobody was going to make a decision for him this time.

He managed to get his face out of the mud and propped himself on his arms. Leaning on his strong left hand, he dragged the other out of the muck and reached for something to hang onto. The hand found a rail or

65

fence post or something of that kind and he grabbed at it to pull himself up. But just as he leaned his weight on it, his fingers let go. The hand hadn't done what he'd wanted. The fingers just slid off the pole and he fell.

He lay in the mud and tried to tell himself he didn't give a good goddamn. He didn't believe it, though. Why should he? Nobody ever believed anything a Meldrin said.

Something was touching his ear. It tickled and he tried to bat at it. He heard the whimper and remembered Dog. Dog was there. Dog was always there. Dog didn't give a damn what his name was or where he'd been or what he'd done. Dog stayed anyway. His hand found Dog's head and scratched it.

He got himself up on his elbows again and then somehow he was on his knees. This time he got the fence post with both hands. It was the corner post of a picket fence. There was lamplight behind a shade in a window and he could see the pickets silhouetted against it. He got himself onto his feet and stood, clinging to the fence.

There was a house back there, behind that fence. As he gazed at the warm glow of the lit window, he saw another light take shape. Someone had opened the door. He saw the figures silhouetted in the doorway. A man and a woman. The man put his arm on her shoulder and kissed her lightly. A real gentlemanly kiss, Clant thought as he watched.

He saw the man jerk down his hat brim and turn to head into the rain. The door closed behind him and his figure was lost in the damp night shadows. But Clant could hear the jangle of his spurs as he crossed the walk.

He heard the creak of the gate hinges and was aware that the man had turned in his direction. Squinting

66

against the rain that stung his eyes, he made out the bulk of the man coming toward him.

He heard the man mutter suddenly, "What the hell?" The voice was Lamar Glynn's.

"Sher'ff?" That was his own voice.

Glynn stopped short. "Clant?"

Clant nodded and shivered at the chill rain that trickled down his spine. He unwrapped one hand from the fence, but his knees felt too weak to take his weight. Looking to Glynn, he said, "Gimme a han', will you, Sher'ff?"

Glynn muttered something under his breath and got Clant's arm over his shoulder. He half-dragged him back toward the house behind the picket fence and around the house to the back door. He knocked hard and after a moment the door panes glowed with lamplight. Then the door swung open.

Clant could see that she was a handsome woman. She stood there in the doorway with the lamp in her hand and looked at them, her forehead creased in anxious puzzlement.

"What is it, Lamar?" she asked. "What's happened?"

"My deputy came back," Glynn grunted.

"Oh."

"I'm sorry, Nora, but . . ."

Clant didn't hear the rest of it.

Slowly he became aware. He became aware that he was warm and dry and naked to the skin under the blanket that was wrapped around him. He became aware that he was sitting at a table gazing down into a half-full cup of black coffee and that his head was nigh to cleaving in two.

He lifted his chin out of his hands and saw Lamar

Glynn sitting across the table from him.

"You feel any better now?" the sheriff asked gruffly.

"I ain't sure," he answered. "How'd I feel before?" He glanced around and saw his clothes hanging over a chair back up near the cook-stove. Dog was lying on the floor in front of the stove in a smear of mud. There was more mud, trekked in from the doorway, spattered on the floor and on the table. It made ugly stains on the crisp white tablecloth. He poked at it with his fingertip. It didn't belong there. It had no damn business being there.

"'Been enjoying yourself?" Glynn said, his voice still hard.

Clant looked at him again. "I stole that bottle."

"It'll damn well come out of your wage, then," Glynn snapped at him.

Resting his head in both hands, he looked down into the coffee cup again. He couldn't remember how long he'd been in the kitchen or how much coffee he'd already had forced down his throat. He knew he wasn't sober enough yet, but he had a sure feeling that if he drank one more mouthful he'd gag on it and be God-awful sick.

"You find anything for me up to Stove Rocks?" Glynn was asking.

With slow, deliberate care, Clant closed his hand on the coffee cup. His right hand. But as he started to lift it, it slipped, hitting the table and almost falling over.

"Easy there," Glynn said, but Clant didn't hear him.

He looked at his hand and at the cup with the coffee sloshing in it. He couldn't quite touch the cup. The thumb and fingers wouldn't quite come together on it.

"Nothing," he said, not looking up. "I didn't find nothing for you. I reckon I ain't know my way around as good as I thought I did."

Glynn sighed. He stubbed out the butt of the cigarette he'd been smoking and leaned back in the chair. "All right, Clant," he said wearily.

"You think I'm lying?" Clant asked. When the sheriff didn't say anything in reply, he figured that was answer enough. "You want me to swear it to you, like that damn deputy's oath?"

"No."

"I'll swear any damn thing you want. My word ain't worth spit."

Glynn sighed again. He said, as if he were explaining something, "You weren't gone very long. Hardly long enough to get up into the Stove Rocks and back. Not long enough to look around any."

"I told you I ain't know where I'm going. I reckon I took a wrong turn or something," Clant insisted.

Glynn started to say something in reply, but instead jerked his head up at the sound of knuckles on the inside door.

The woman's voice came through the panels: "Is it all right for me to come in, Lamar?"

Glynn shot a glance at Clant and saw him wrap a hand over the edges of the blanket, pulling it closer across his bare chest. "Come ahead, Nora," he called back to her.

The door cracked slightly and then swung open, and the woman stepped in. The look she gave to Clant was sharp-edged with disapproval.

"You'll excuse me, ma'am, if I don't stand up?" Clant said to her with a twisted grin as he tightened his grip on the blanket.

"Clant," Glynn growled, down deep in his throat, like a dog giving a warning.

69

But it wasn't the sheriff's threat that backed him down. He looked at the woman with her scrubbed face and her frilly dress all crisp and clean. As clean as the tablecloth had been before he'd spattered mud on it. This was *her* house, he realized. It was *her* fire in the stove, *her* coffee, and *her* blanket that was warm and dry on his shoulders. He wondered what he was doing here, in a place like this, and he asked her, "You ain't know me?"

"You're Clant Meldrin," she said. She said it like it was any name, like it was just a handle hung onto a man so's a person could grab hold of his attention by it.

But that wasn't so, he thought. From the look in her eyes she did know him—at least by reputation. And still he was sitting at *her* table with the warm blanket around him. It seemed like there was something he should say. Something he couldn't recall ever having said before. He cast about in his mind for the words. He looked down into the coffee cup but there was no answer there. "Look here," he began and that sounded really wrong. Lamely, he muttered, "I know better'n I behave."

"Don't apologize," she snapped.

He looked at her again, feeling the bite of her words like a whip. The blanket be damned, he thought. He damn well hadn't asked her for it. He hadn't asked her for anything. "If you'll go 'way so's I can get dressed, I'll get the hell out'n your house," he said. Then he added viciously, "Or stay and watch if you want."

She was shocked enough to satisfy him. But then the look in her eyes changed. There was something sad in her voice as she said, "No, I think you're wrong, Clant Meldrin. I don't think you do know any better than you behave. I don't think you're even housebroken." She moved her eyes to Glynn and the look she gave him was

70

as if she'd reached out and put a hand on his shoulder. Like she meant to comfort him in some sorrow.

"I reckon he's sober enough now," Glynn said to her, as if he were answering a question. "I'll take him back where he belongs."

"Jail?" Clant asked.

"Is that where you figure you belong?" Glynn countered.

Clant's head throbbed. He rested it in his hands again as he muttered, "I ain't know where I belong."

The silence was long and Clant began to get the feeling that he was completely alone. He started to look up just as Glynn said, "You're gonna have to sleep in the jail tonight. I can't haul you into any respectable boardinghouse the shape you're in."

"I ain't care where I sleep," he mumbled in reply. "Not so long as the door ain't locked."

He heard Glynn say, "Nora, I'd better get him dressed and take him out of here."

Her voice soft with concern, she answered, "Take care of yourself, Lamar."

Clant looked over his fingertips at her as she turned and walked out of the room. It seemed like a funny thing for her to have said. He frowned, puzzling over it. She sure as hell couldn't know about Isham, could she?

"Can you dress yourself?" the sheriff said, getting up.

"I reckon," he answered, and Glynn flung his drawers at him. He caught them, but when he tried to stand up he discovered that he wasn't as close to sober as he'd thought. He didn't have much control over either hand and even his legs didn't seem to work so well. Moving set his head to spinning and his thoughts blurred and ran together at the edges. But somehow he managed to get his pants on and then the shirt. Once that was done, the vest was easy enough. He sat down again to fight his way into the boots. And that seemed to be all of it. Or was it? He had a vague feeling something was missing.

"Where's my gun?" he asked.

"You weren't wearing one," Glynn said.

"Weren't I?" He considered that. Dammit, it was getting harder and harder to think. If only he could put his head down and sleep for a while—what was it Glynn had just told him? He remembered.

"No," he agreed, "I ain't never wear a gun no more."

"Why not?" he asked himself. Hell, he'd always worn a gun. It was the one thing he was handy with, the one thing his pap had took pride in him for.

He answered his own question aloud. "Man wears a gun, he's got to mind out or it might be he'll use it. 'Specially if his hand moves quicker'n he thinks. Somebody up and provoke him and he use it, next thing he know some ol' judge is sayin', 'Meldrin, boy, you goin' home for a long time. A damn long time.' And I ain't care is home six foot of pine box or just that same ol' pen'tentiary, I ain't want to go there." He rested his face in his hands again. "Damn you, Isham. I ain't want to go back."

Somebody had hold of his shoulder. Isham? He made a move to push away the hand as he looked up. But he missed. And it wasn't Isham. He said, "I know you, Lamar Glynn."

"Sure you do," the sheriff said. "You reckon you can walk?"

He nodded.

"Come on, boy," Glynn said.

Clant dragged himself to his feet. "Don't you call me that! You call me that, I'll kill you without I think twice about it!"

72

Glynn shook his head slowly, as would a man who has a good-sized job in front of him and who's trying to figure out just where to lay hold of it. He jerked Clant's arm over his shoulder and started him toward the door.

"Where's Dog," Clant mumbled. "I ain't go nowhere without Dog."

CHAPTER 7

SOMEHOW NORA ELLISON WAS ALL TANGLED UP IN Clant's dreams. And when he woke, she was still in his mind. His recollection of the night before and of having been in her kitchen was blurred and muddled. But he remembered that he'd drunk her coffee, warmed himself at her fire, and left her home filthy with the mud he'd wallowed in. He had a strong feeling that he should apologize somehow.

He ate in the café against the county bill. The breakfast didn't interest him much, but the coffee took the edge off his thirst. On the way back to the sheriff's office, he stopped in the mercantile to get another plug of tobacco against his bill and managed to talk Langer into letting him have a new hat as well. But that was the last of his credit, the shopkeeper warned him. Not one more plug until he paid up. He headed back to the office, hoping he'd find Glynn there and be able to talk him out of some cash money, but when he got there the sheriff was gone.

He walked on into the cell where he'd slept for two nights and began digging into his war bag. As he flung the spare shirt onto the bunk and rummaged for the razor, he thought to himself that the cell was turning into his home in Jubilee. Well, as long as the door stood

73

open . . . He found the razor and then slung the shirt over his shoulder and headed out to find water.

Remembering Lady's prodding, he intended to shave and clean himself up before he went calling. He knew that Lady was sometimes wrong in her notions about proper manners, but pretty often she was right and he owned that she knew a damn sight more about it that he did.

Finally, with the dried mud brushed off his britches and boots and with the new hat set on the back of his head, he set out to find the house behind the picket fence.

When he found it, he halted himself on the front steps. He had a notion it might be wiser to knock at the back door instead. He could scent fresh baking as he walked around the house and when the door was opened to his knock the aroma hit him in the face. It was apple pie with cinnamon in it, and it smelled a sight more interesting than café grub. He breathed deeply of it and then drew his attention back to the reason he'd come.

Nora Ellison stood there in the doorway, wiping her flour-smeared hands on her apron. The cornflower blue housedress she wore was neat and trim, but her hair had begun to work loose from the ribbon that gathered it and loose strands wandered down over her forehead. It set off her face with its softness.

Looking at her here in the morning sunlight, he judged her to be about his own age. And a damn handsome woman. But she didn't look like a very friendly one. The steps up into the kitchen gave her an advantage of height, and she added to it by straightening her shoulders and stiffening her spine as she looked down at him.

"What do you want?" she said coldly.

"I'm sorry." It was all he could think of to say. He turned to walk away.

"Wait a minute," she called to him.

He turned back and looked at her questioningly.

"Did Lamar send you here to apologize?" she asked.

"No," he admitted.

She smiled. It did wonderful things to her face and somehow he found himself grinning back at her. For a few minutes there he'd felt like a damned fool coming to the house this way. But looking at her smile, he got the notion that maybe she wasn't going to hold it against him.

Nora brushed at the hair that straggled out of the ribbon as she studied over the young man who'd knocked at her door. He dressed like some grubline rider, in range clothes that were worn and weathered beyond being of any particular color, except for the incongruously new hat. But there was no gun on his hip. Shaved and scrubbed and in the light of morning, he didn't really look much like an outlaw. Not with the hat in his hands and his fingers working nervously over the stiff edge of the brim that way. He had a kind of shy, crooked grin that put her in mind of a schoolboy about to offer to carry some young lady's books for her.

And she remembered something Lamar had said the night before, when he had dragged the filthy, drunken carcass of Clant Meldrin into her kitchen. "The years a body's got on him don't necessarily make a man of him," Lamar had said. "There's some as grow up young and some as never make it at all, no matter how long they live."

When she'd thought about that, she'd decided she was one of the ones who'd grown up young. Married at sixteen and widowed by twenty—suddenly out here in

75

the wilderness with no family this side of the river—she'd had to make her own way in the world.

Before the fever had taken her husband, he had built this home, and he had loved this country. She'd come to love it, too, and with the house and the little money he'd left her, she'd determined to stay on. She'd always been handy with needle and thread and in the three years since he'd died, she'd managed to make her small business successful.

And she'd fallen in love with Lamar Glynn.

As hard as life had been, she thought, it was still a good life. With Lamar, it would go on being a good life.

Standing in the doorway looking at Clant Meldrin, she told herself that if she intended to share her life with Lamar, she had to share his troubles with him as well. And this strange young man was important to Lamar. Therefore he was important to her, and she had to help Lamar with him in whatever way she could.

She wiped her hands on her apron and said, "I have a couple of pies just out of the oven. They're from a new recipe I haven't used before. I wonder if you'd care to give me an opinion on them."

He nodded. Like a shy schoolboy, she thought as she stepped back from the doorway. "Won't you come inside? There's coffee on the stove."

He started in and the dog started after him. "No," he said to the animal. "You ain't better come."

Dog hesitated and gave a tentative wag of his tail.

"He won't do any harm," Nora said.

Clant clicked his tongue and the dog bounded joyfully up the steps after him.

Nora came back with a big slice of pie on a china plate then set a cup in front of him. He looked at it and at the tablecloth. It was different from the one he

76

remembered. The other had been all white with shiny threads making patterns in it. This one was checkered, pale blue and white, and stiff with starch. It was spotlessly clean.

He looked down at the floor. The planks had been thoroughly scrubbed. There was no sign of mud, no trace of the filth he'd brought in the night before. He thought to himself that he must have left her a real job of work when Glynn herded him out. It seemed uncommon sociable of her not to at least cuss him out for it.

She bent over the table as she tilted the coffeepot over the cup. She was so close that he could smell the clean soap-scent of her. His eyes went to the line of her bosom.

She wasn't round and jiggly like Angel, but firmly full-breasted. A growed woman and a damn handsome one, he thought to himself. Her throat was slender and white, her face soft and smooth with no flaky wrinkling from the weather. And there was no paint on her mouth. The color was natural. The lips were just full enough, like berries turning ripe and tartly sweet.

"Uncommon sociable," he thought, and he asked himself why else would she have invited him into the kitchen like this—especially after the way he'd carried on the night before? He remembered the words he'd thrown at her to shock her. Well, maybe that hadn't been shock he'd seen in her face then. Maybe Glynn was a mite too much of a gentleman for a full-growed woman.

As she set the coffeepot back on the stove, he rose and closed a hand around her wrist. He jerked her toward him, wrapping the other arm around her waist, feeling the warmth of her body under the dress. He

77

caught her mouth hard with his.

She struggled against him the way Angel did. No, he realized with surprise, she wasn't playing the way Angel did. She was really trying to get free of him. He eased his hold on her.

She moved suddenly, pulling free of his grip and swinging.

Clant winced. He stumbled back at the stab of pain in his face. That wasn't just her hand she'd swung at him. It felt like fire. A stove lid clattered on the floor at his feet.

He raised his eyes to the girl. She had backed away from him, backed herself into a corner. She stood half-crouched with the lid holder still in her hand, raised like a club. Her knuckles were white with tension and her face as pale as flour.

He could see easily enough what had happened. She'd grabbed the first thing under her hand and heaved it at him. It had been the stove lid, hot off the fire, and it had caught him edge on, across the side of his jaw.

He put his hand to his face, cupping his palm over the burn. It hurt. He said, "I reckon that weren't what you wanted."

"You stay away from me," she shouted, her voice almost breaking.

"I ain't touch you again," he muttered. With his right hand, he picked up his hat and slapped it onto his head.

The frown that came over her face made a small crease between her eyes. She looked at the stove lid on the floor and then at the hand he held cupped over his jaw. "Are you hurt?" she asked.

"No."

She took a shaky, tentative step toward him. And then a firm step as if she'd gathered rein on her fear. For an

78

instant he thought she meant to start flailing at him with the lid handle. But she threw it down. Putting her fingers on his wrist, she nudged at the hand he held against his face as she said, "Let me see."

He let her move his hand. The frown-crease deepened as she looked at his jaw. "Sit down," she said. It was an order.

Bewildered, he sat down.

She turned to the work counter and when she turned back she had a lump of butter on her fingertips. "Here," she muttered as she dabbed it over the burn.

Then she stepped away from him again, backing up and wiping her hands on her apron. Her breath was still short and there wasn't much color in her face yet, but there was no fear left in it, either. She looked at him in the same cold-eyed disapproving way she had the night before and said, "No. *That* wasn't what I wanted."

It took him a moment to recall the words she was answering. Apologetically, he told her, "I ain't know no better."

She raised an eyebrow slightly, as if she didn't believe him, and snapped, "Well, you do now."

He nodded.

"Now get out!" She pointed a finger toward the door.

As he got to his feet, he asked, "That was about the wrongest thing I could of done?"

"Yes."

He paused at the doorway. "Then how come you invite me into your kitchen the way you done?"

"I forgot you aren't housebroken." Her voice was still whip-sharp.

"Do any good I say I'm sorry?" he asked.

She shook her head.

It was true though, he thought. He felt like hell about

79

it. He felt more damn rotten miserable than he could make sense of. Slowly, reluctant to leave without having made amends somehow, he pushed the door open and clicked his tongue at Dog.

Dog walked slowly too, with his tail down, as if he felt some kind of guilt at her anger. He nosed at Clant's leg and made a small noise deep in his throat.

Clant stopped on the bottom step and looked back again. Nora was still standing there with her hands on her hips, still gazing at him in that knife-edged way.

He rubbed his knuckles on the edge of the butter-smear on his jaw and said, "I'm obliged for the grease."

Suddenly, astonishingly, the steel went out of her eyes and the corners of her mouth turned in that small smile. "Darn you, Clant Meldrin," she said, but it wasn't even hardly angry.

He looked at her, not understanding.

"You aren't setting foot back in my house," she said sternly. "But I promised you a piece of pie. If you still want it you can sit there on the steps and eat it."

He realized that in some strange woman-way she was accepting his apology. She wasn't exactly backing down, but she wasn't running him off either.

"I'd be obliged," he said.

As she went back into the kitchen, he settled himself on the step. Dog put a paw up on his knee and looked at him hopefully.

"It's all right, feller," he said as he scrubbed his fingers into the animal's neck hair. Dog seemed satisfied.

Nora came back with a big slice of pie on a china plate and a cup of coffee in her other hand. She gave them to Clant and turned away.

He didn't want her to go back behind that door.

80

Maybe if he behaved himself she'd stay and talk a while. "You know Lamar Glynn long, ma'am?" he asked her.

"Not as long as you have."

"I ain't know him at all," he mumbled.

"He said he knew you in Missouri."

"Maybe. But I ain't know him." He cut at the pie with the fork she'd given him. It was an awkward eating tool, not nearly as handy as his sheath knife. But he felt he should stick with it while she was watching. He looked at her and asked, "He told you about me?"

She nodded very slightly. Cocking her head a bit, she asked conversationally, "Does your dog have a name?"

"I ain't know," he said. "He ain't belong to me. We're just traveling together."

"Why don't you give him a name?"

"Ain't my business to. Like I said, he ain't *belong* to me. He belong to himself." He gulped at the coffee and then told her, "A man gets give a name and he's stuck with it. I reckon it might be the same way with a dog. I got no right to hang no name on him."

She couldn't figure out just what he meant. But from the way he'd said it, she knew he put a lot of importance on names. She asked him, "Is Clant your whole name?"

"Clanton Meldrin," he answered her. "Pap didn't know enough Christian names to give us all two apiece." He sampled the pie. It was still too hot for eating so he went on talking. "They was thirteen of us, counting the ones that didn't live to grow up. I was the last one and he took my name off some kind of a handbill. Reward dodger, I think it was, for a feller name of Willie Clanton. Only he already had a Willie in the family."

She smiled again. "*What* about your mother?" she

81

asked.

He wasn't sure what she meant. *What* about his mother? He said, "I ain't recall her too good. She died when we was on the way to Missouri from Georgia."

He tried the pie again. It was almost cool enough now for eating. He stuffed a piece into his mouth. When he'd swallowed, he said thoughtfully, "Funny thing, though, Ma was a fair-educated woman. I ain't know how she ever took up with the likes of Pap."

"She loved him," Nora suggested.

He nodded. "She must of. And him her, too. They was proper married, by a preacher and all that, with papers. That ain't none too common in the Meldrin family."

"Do you know her maiden name?" she asked.

"Her what?"

"Her family name before she was married."

He thought for a moment. "Jones, I think. She was from up to the Carolinas but I ain't sure which one. She was a good looking woman and right educated. She could read books and figure and play the mouth harp and dulcimer and guitar, all real good. She made lace, too."

"Did she teach you?"

"To make lace?" he scowled at her.

She laughed. It was a warm, pleasant laugh. "No, I mean to read. Lamar said you could."

"I reckon I can," he nodded. "What reading I got, I learnt off my brother Bob. She learnt him how but I weren't old enough then."

"And writing?"

"Bob could write up a fair hand. He even went to school a mite before Ma died. I ain't never got the hang of it though." He flexed the fingers of his right hand. "I

82

set myself out to learn how once but I kinda got interrupted in my lessons. Never learnt to deal cards worth a damn neither."

"Is dealing cards something you have to learn?"

"Dealing the ones you want where you want 'em is. That was my brother Zeb's best skill. Each us boys had some skill he took his pride in and tried to outdo the rest with. Zeb, it was his hands. You never seen a pair of hands could move no more smoother nor slicker than his. Hell, I reckon he could even of made lace if he'd took a notion to."

Smiling again, she asked, "What was your special skill?"

"Handgun," he answered. "All us boys had to be handy with guns. Pap set a lot of store by it. Nigh time I was big enough to hold up a horse pistol, I set into learning." He opened and closed his fingers again, studying them. "Pistol shooting don't take but one hand. And I showed the whole damn lot of 'em a few things about using a gun. That was afore I'd got my growth, too." He forked the last piece of the pie into his mouth.

The answer she'd gotten disturbed Nora. The matter-of-fact way he'd given it to her bothered her. She wondered at the job Lamar had taken on himself in the taming of Clant Meldrin. But perhaps a woman's hand was needed she thought. Lamar would need all the help she could give him. She cast about for some constructive suggestion.

"If you can read, you could learn to write easily enough," she said.

"I ain't know about that." He set the pie plate down on the step and looked at both his hands. He'd never used the left one for anything much until the time he'd torn up the other one. Learning to use it at all hadn't been easy. And when he'd tried to hold a slate pencil with it and follow the copybook his brother had worked him from, the results had been so damn miserable that Bob had just plain lost patience and told him to go to hell. After that, he hadn't bothered much with trying.

Almost as if she could read his thoughts, she said, "If you can handle a gun you can handle a pen."

It was like an accusation. It was like Glynn prodding at him. Or like Isham throwing orders at him. He got to his feet and touched the brim of his hat. "I'm obliged for the pie and coffee, ma'am."

"Are you going to try at all, Clant Meldrin?" she called after him. "Or are you just going to hang around taking advantage of Lamar's generosity?"

"Maybe I ain't hang around much longer," he muttered under his breath as he turned into the street. With the dog trotting along at his heels, he headed back toward the jailhouse.

As he walked, he worked at a quid of the Dan Webster. It eased his thirst a bit, but it didn't ease his mind at all. He felt as though he'd been strung up to the post with Isham whipping him from one side and Glynn and his woman from the other. There didn't seem to be anything else to do but saddle up and get the hell away from all of them.

When he walked into the sheriff's office, Glynn was there, behind the desk, figuring with a pencil at some kind of paperwork. The sheriff looked up at him and asked, "What'd you do to your face?"

Clant touched his fingertips lightly to the burn. It stung. "Cut m'self shaving," he mumbled.

"You shave with a running iron?" Glynn said.

"Not generally," he answered, and headed on into the cell. Dropping himself down on the bunk, he stuck his

84

hands under his head and gazed at the ceiling.

If he intended to saddle up and get, he asked himself, why wasn't he doing it? He couldn't name himself one single good reason to stay on in Jubilee. Nor was there any reason to go back to Fairweather and Isham—not any good one. The thing to do was head south, the way he'd intended when he'd bought the horse. There was nothing to hold him from it.

He thought of Isham. He hadn't promised Ish he'd take part in the robbery. He hadn't even agreed to spy on the sheriff the way Ish had ordered. What cause did Ish have to expect him to go through with it anyway? He'd warned his brother that he was cutting his own trail now.

And why the hell did he have to fight it out with himself? Why didn't he just climb on board that dun horse and get?

He thought about the horse. Why the hell did a horse let itself get reined and rode anyway? Natural thing for a horse was to tear around wild, going where it wanted, eating when it pleased, and tossing its heels in the air. But let somebody throw a rope on a horse, haul it down, and cinch a saddle on its back. Let him give it a good hard fight or two and before long that horse'd come to the notion to do what it was told. Maybe it would keep on fussing and fighting now and then, shaking out kinks in the morning and trying to duck loops in the corral. But under a firm hand it'd settle down and answer the rein.

A saddle and spurs, though, reins and a spade bit, those were things that could be seen and felt, same as leg irons and a bullwhip. And a horse that shows fight, you have to keep it hobbled or tied. You couldn't turn it loose and expect to have it stand and do as it's told. If you give it half a chance it'll bunch up and light out without a notion of ever letting you set a rope on it again.

What about a man, then? Why would a man stand to be saddled and rode without somebody had a rope on him? Why would he go against his own feelings and do as he was told without somebody ever laying a whip to him? What kind of a hold could one man get over another that he'd answer sure as a Spanish spade even though he hated it as much as a horse must hate a high-port bit?

The jangle of Lamar Glynns spurs and the thud of his heels interrupted Clant's thoughts. He looked up as the sheriff walked in.

"Clant, you in trouble?" Glynn asked him.

"No more'n usual, I ain't think," he answered.

"Why?"

The sheriff pulled the straight-back chair away from the wall a bit and settled himself into it. He started assembling a quirly and Clant knew that he was assembling his thoughts, too. Glynn had some kind of question in his mind that he meant to circle up on the back way.

Clant had a sudden picture in his mind of himself backed into a corral corner with Glynn working up on him, a loop in one hand and a bridle in the other.

"You're sure?" Glynn asked.

Maybe it was the burn on his face that the sheriff was concerned over, he thought. He touched his fingers to it and said, "It was a lady that done it."

"Huh?"

"Was a lady. She hit me in the face with a stove lid."

Glynn grinned a bit. "I didn't know any of your ladyfriends got up this early."

86

Clant sat up slowly, working the stub of railroad spike out of his pocket as he did. He had that damned ornery feeling and he knew he was going to bust loose and do some stomping before he let himself get ridden this time. "Wasn't one of mine," he said with deliberation. "It was your'n."

The grin went off Glynn's face. "What do you mean by that?"

"I went calling on our ladyfriend this morning. That Nora Ellison. She's a lot of woman, ain't she?" He spat tobacco juice and wiped his mouth with the back of his hand.

Glynn came up out of the chair. But instead of lunging, he wheeled. Without a word, he hurried to the door and out, into the street.

Clant got up and ambled to the doorway. Leaning a shoulder against the frame, he worked the plug out of his pocket and bit off a chunk as he watched the sheriff striding in the direction of the house behind the picket fence. Damn strange thing, he thought. He couldn't make sense of Glynn. He'd been so sure the sheriff would jump him, or maybe even throw down on him.

Turning, he unpinned the star from his vest and tossed it onto the desk. Then he went into the cell and stuffed a few loose belongings into the war bag. As he started back through the office with it over his shoulder, he paused and looked at the badge. He had a strange notion he wanted to keep it. As a souvenir, he told himself. The story of Clant Meldrin, Lawman, ought to be good for a few laughs and a few free drinks somewhere along the road.

He picked up the badge and stuffed it into his vest pocket. Four days at a dollar a day—well, the hat alone was priced at more'n that. And besides the hat he'd had a few plugs of Dan'l Webster charged against his account, not to mention the bottle he'd stolen from the Grand Pacific Palace.

Remembering the bottle put him in mind that he wanted a drink before he hit the trail. And something to carry along for a cold night's camping. He still had the two-bit piece, but that wasn't near enough. Nowhere near enough. He glanced around the office; wondering if the sheriff kept either a bottle or a little loose change lying around.

There was a short coat hung on a wall peg. Likely Glynn's, he thought as he went through the pockets. He came up with odds and ends but no money.

Returning to the desk, he began to rummage through the drawers. Maybe the sheriff kept something there that a barkeep would take in pawn.

Nothing inside the desk looked worth the trouble he'd taken hunting through it. For sure none of it would interest anyone into trading a drink or two. Seating himself in the swivel chair, Clant began to count off his belongings on his fingertips, trying to figure what he owned that he could pawn and would be willing to part with.

Curiously, he looked over the stuff on the desk—the papers sheriff Glynn had been working on. Nothing of interest, just some kind of report about tax collections. But the sheriff wrote a real neat copybook hand.

Clant picked up the pencil. Holding it in his left hand, he made a looping scrawl on the paper. It wiggled like a snake on a hot rock. He shifted the pencil to his right hand. The fingers closed on it, all right, but it felt even more awkward than it did in his left. He jabbed at the paper with it a couple of times and then shifted it back to the other hand.

He tried a copybook exercise he remembered vaguely, a long line of coils. They wouldn't come out even. The line wavered and he discovered that he had to crane his wrist around and hold his hand above the line to see what kind of marks he was making on the paper.

He made a stab at writing his name. Not the lumpy squiggle he'd used the few times he'd had to put his mark to something, but each letter laid out proper. He wasn't exactly satisfied with the results, but at least it could be read back. Second time he tried, it didn't come out as good as the first. But by the fifth try, he'd decided that he was beginning to get the hang of it. He made a broad bold slash across the top of the *t* and hit the dot over the *i* a good hard whomp. It broke the point of the pencil. A couple of quick licks with his sheath knife put a fresh point on it and he tried again.

By the time he'd filled in all the space on the margins of the sheet, he was feeling fairly pleased with himself. He turned the paper over. The whole backside of it was bare and challenging. That gave him the notion to try something harder than just a two-piece name. He pondered a while for something fancier to write but nothing came to mind, so he dug around on the desk for something to copy. He came up with the oath Glynn had used to swear him in when he'd gotten the deputy's badge.

It took a piece of studying before he started and once he got to copying it, he spent more time chewing on the point of the pencil and staring at the papers than he did making marks. He'd gotten himself completely engrossed in the problem and didn't even notice the footsteps. It wasn't until a shadow fell across the worksheet that he realized someone was looking at him. He jerked his head up guiltily, embarrassed at having

89

been caught at what he was doing. Crumpling the paper in his hand, he tossed it on the floor.

The man standing across the desk from him was a rannihan he'd seen around a few times. He'd never gotten a name attached to the face, but he had a vague recollection of him being one of the Jay-Bar crew.

"What do you want?" he snapped.

The Jay-Bar man looked taken aback. "Sheriff Glynn," he said. "He around here somewheres?"

"Over to the Widder Ellison's, I reckon," Clant answered sharply. "That's where he looked headed, last I seen of him."

"Obliged," the Jay-Bar man mumbled. He touched his hat brim to Clant and walked out.

Once the man was gone, Clant got to his feet and flung the pencil away from him. He gathered up the war bag and headed out. So there wasn't enough money for drinking-liquor. He'd traveled dry before. There was a sound horse, a bait of supplies left from his trip up to Stove Rocks, and a lot of land to be covered before he'd reach the far side of the Llano Estacado.

CHAPTER 8

IT WAS A DECENT ENOUGH DAY FOR TRAVELING. THE sky was overcast, so there was no sun to warm the autumn chill out of the air. But there wasn't any rain.

Dog ranged out, chasing varmints as usual and racing back now and then to let Clant know he hadn't lit a shuck or gotten himself lost or anything like that. The dun horse moved on at a good, easy, ground-covering pace.

As he rode, Clant amused himself by singing. It

helped him keep thoughts from busting into his mind. And the dun horse didn't seem to object any. Like any good animal that's worked night herd, it cocked its ears back, bobbed its head, and relaxed, certain that as long as the rider was making those same strange noises all was well with the world. This particular rider sang louder than a night-herder, but the sounds had the same reassuring monotony.

" 'Farewell, Mother, for you'll never see my name among the slain, For if I can just skedaddle, Mother, I'll come home again . . .' "

Clant didn't stop to make camp until he had crossed the creek that marked the county line. It was well into night by then, and downright cold. But there was no reason why he couldn't build a decent fire. He sat close up to it with the saddle blanket across his shoulders to keep the wind off, and as he gazed at the flames, he got to asking himself why he hadn't hocked something and bought a bottle.

He could have traded off that old Remington handgun. He sure as hell didn't need it, did he? What was the use of owning a gun you kept in your war bag and never used but for sneaking off in the back meadows and proving to yourself that you could still handle it?

He'd thought about selling the revolver before. He'd even decided a time or two that he would. But when it came right down to doing it, he'd always backed out with the uncomfortable feeling that it would be like selling the hand off of his arm. He recalled something one of the missionaries to the prison had said once that had stuck in his mind: " 'And if thy right hand offend thee, cut it off and cast it from thee.' "

He looked at his hands in the flickering light of the

fire. Hell, that right hand was something he could do without easy enough. All it had ever done for him was get him in trouble. And the left hand? "If thy gun hand offend thee, sell thy gun and buy drinking liquor with the money," he thought.

What was the left hand good for except throwing a gun?

Just once more, he thought, if just this once more he'd pick up that gun—hell, all he'd have to do would be put a couple of slugs into that sheriff, Lamar Glynn, and he'd be putting enough money into his hand to buy a damn lot of liquor. A hell of a lot more than he could trade an old cap-and-ball revolver for. The gun without his hand on it wouldn't be worth much. And his hand without the gun in it?

He pulled out the plug of Dan'l Webster and gnawed off a chunk. As he stuffed it back into his pocket, he thought of the two-bit piece. That was hardly even tobacco money.

He picked up a stick and poked at the fire, sending spiral of sparks up in the rising smoke. Man couldn't do that if he got himself outlawed, he told himself. He'd have to be damn careful about showing his fire—or his face either, for that matter.

Man got himself outlawed, he'd likely end up out on the back trails with Fairweather and his boys or some other bunch of the same kind, taking chances and taking orders. Either that or he'd go it alone, jumping every time he heard a twig crack and wrapping his hand around a gun every time he saw a shadow move. Else maybe he'd get himself caught and shoveled back into a penitentiary or a hole in the ground.

He worked the quid, spat in the fire, and then banked it and wrapped himself in the blanket. The wind swept down the valley and he pulled the blanket tight against it. Wind didn't stop at a county line. Neither did a man's thoughts.

Dawn came gray and cold and edged with low clouds. Clant sat huddled close to the fire as he boiled coffee. It didn't look to shape up into much of a day. Maybe it wouldn't rain and maybe the dampness in the air wouldn't thicken into snow, but it still didn't look to shape up into much of a day.

The coffee was thick and bitter. It burned in his throat but it didn't take the chill off his innards. It only set him in mind of the coffee he'd drunk at Nora Ellison's. Sweet coffee and hot pie, cut with a fork. Man could probably get the hang of using a fork easy enough. Pushing a pencil hadn't turned out to be as hard as he'd expected, not once he put his mind to it. Maybe next chance he got, he'd get hold of a pencil and some paper and practice up on that a mite. Show that damn sheriff and his woman that he could learn a thing if he tried.

But that was what Glynn had been saying, wasn't it? It was the direction Glynn had been trying to herd him in. And besides, dammit, he had no plans to ever run into the sheriff again, either. The more distance he could put between Glynn and himself, the happier he'd be. Still, it might be fun—he could get practiced and then write a letter and mail it off to the sheriff.

Only there wouldn't be much point in that after the first of the month. Fairweather and Isham and the boys would be leaving a few corpses when they rode out of Jubilee with that bank money. Sure as hell, Lamar Glynn would be one of them. Glynn was the kind who'd butt in to stop them and who'd stand to fight until one of them dropped him.

Clant counted days on his fingers. He had a notion it would be a good idea to get himself into a town on the first of the month and make sure he was seen there. Maybe even get himself jailed for a few days. In all the confusion of a bank raid folks can get mistaken ideas of what they see. Those folks back in Jubilee knew him by sight, and he knew how much he and Isham resembled each other. It would be easy enough for one to be mistaken for the other in the excitement.

Dammit, getting mixed up with Fairweather this time hadn't been his idea. Like that Jay-Bar rider, he'd just stumbled across the outlaw when he was hunting strays. And Fairweather had soft-talked him into trying to root up a little information in town, offering him a real good price for it. Only Paul didn't pay off and now . . . He bit a chunk from the plug and got to his feet. Now he had to saddle up and get moving.

He was going to have to put distance between himself and Isham, too. Ish would be right riled to learn he'd run but. And Ish wasn't one to put up with nonsense, especially not from a kid brother. Once he'd pocketed his share of the bank money, it was fair likely he'd start looking for his kid brother with the plan of learning him who was boss in what was left of the Meldrin family. If Isham ever got a rope on him after this, he'd damn sure crop his ears.

Clant put a hand to his earlobe as he thought about that. If it ever came to Isham's mind, it was just the kind of damn fool meanness he might really do. Down in parts of the country where there wasn't much law, when folks caught up with a rustler and decided for some reason not to string him up, they'd crop his ears—same as they would a calf. It marked him for what he was the same way. When folks would see a man had his ears

94

cropped, they'd read his brand and know him for a thief. He'd have a hard time getting hired onto a riding job. Or likely any other job either. Man can't get work, he ends up riding the back trails with a bunch like Fairweather's—likely that'd suit Isham real fine.

Ain't supposed to be a man could own another like you'd own a horse or a beef. That was part of what the war was about, the way he'd heard it. Abe Lincoln had freed the slaves and no man could put his brand on another anymore. Not under the law. But what the hell was the law to a Meldrin? And there were other ways to own a man besides you held title papers on him. You just plain back him into a corner where they ain't no way he can run and nothing he can do but what you tell him.

Clant drew rein on the dun and shifted in the saddle, looking back at the hills behind him. The clouds hung low and gray over them. Wasn't nothing back there toward Jubilee but trouble, he told himself. And likely wasn't nothing up ahead but trouble either. Whichever way he turned he'd be either riding straight into it or running with it close on his tail. That much at least, he was damn sure of.

He worked the plug out of his pocket and bit off a piece. Two bits in his pocket, he told himself as he closed his jaws on it. That wouldn't hardly keep him in tobacco till he got across the plain.

He worked the wad a while; then he tucked it into his cheek and gave a whistle that brought Dog racing toward him. Then he laid rein against the dun's neck and turned back toward Jubilee.

It was well into the night when he reached Jubilee, and the town had pretty much closed down. He had to

95

pound at the stable door to wake the swamper. The old man grumbled at being wakened but made no objection to Clant's bedding the horse against the county bill. Maybe the sheriff had forgotten to spread the word about how his new deputy had walked off the payroll.

He found the sheriffs office dark and the door locked. After rattling the knob a couple of times, and getting no response, he turned to look up and down the empty street. Glynn stayed at one of the boarding houses, but he'd never bothered to find out which one. Only maybe Glynn hadn't gone home yet. Maybe he'd gone calling.

He shouldered his war bag and headed toward Nora Ellison's house. He found it easy enough, but there was no light showing anywhere. Cutting through the yard, he made a full circle around the house to be sure, but not a window showed a trace of light.

That didn't prove the sheriff wasn't there, he figured. But it was reason enough to leave them be. When a man was as soon to be dead as Lamar Glynn likely was, he should be let to take his pleasure without interruption.

He set off to hunt up an open shed or empty stall somewhere to bed himself down in for the night.

Nora Ellison was troubled in her mind. Usually she didn't worry much about Lamar Glynn. A lot of men did jobs every bit as dangerous as a lawman's. A cowhand or a railroad man, a soldier or a miner, could get himself hurt or killed easily enough. And Lamar was competent at his work.

But the idea of the outlaw gang hidden up on the mountain and of Lamar riding up there by himself— even if he did only mean to spy around and then ride back again—it worried her. And there was Clant Meldrin with his boyish grin and his murderous

96

reputation—she recalled how Lamar had told her a day might come when he would have to kill Clant Meldrin.

She'd gone to bed early, but she hadn't slept well at all. Come morning, though, she'd taken her time in front of the mirror, confronting her image in it as she brushed out her hair. She'd bolstered her courage with brave thoughts and assurances that Lamar knew exactly what he was doing and could handle himself in any situation that might arise.

Feeling almost satisfied, almost confident, she'd finished putting her hair up and had gone to the kitchen to set herself a cup of coffee. She hummed a cheery tune as she poured it and put it on the table. Then she replaced the pot on the stove and was about to sit down, when she heard the knock at the door.

Puzzled at who could be calling this early, she swung it open. She found herself facing Clant Meldrin.

The sight of him startled her—and frightened her. He stood at the bottom of the steps, dirty and unshaven and working a cud of tobacco in his jaws. And there was nothing of the shy schoolboy in his face as he looked at her this time.

He tucked the quid into his cheek. Glancing past her into the kitchen, he said, "I'm looking for Sheriff Glynn."

The implication in his words angered her more than the look of him had frightened her. She snapped indignantly, "He isn't *here!*"

"Where is he?" The bland way he had asked was irritating.

"Looking for you," she answered, as if it were a threat.

"Why?" He seemed surprised.

"To kill you!"

He frowned slightly and spat tobacco juice into the flower bed by the doorstep. Looking back at Nora, he asked, "Why he want to kill me? Just on account of I wouldn't stand peaceable to be bridled?"

"He thought you went—" she broke off and studied him. Remembering what Lamar had said about the trip up to the mountain, she counted days mentally. Her voice calmer, more controlled, she asked, "Where *did* you go?"

"I run off," he said. "But I'm back now. Where'd he think I went?"

She didn't give him any reply.

"Up to Stove Rocks?" he asked.

She nodded then. And asked, "But you didn't go back there?"

"No, ma'am. What give him the notion I'd went off to the Stove Rocks?"

"He heard about your brother being with Fairweather. Then you disappeared. And after the way you'd lied to him, what was he to think?"

"He knows I've seen brother Isham up there?"

"He figured it out. One of the Jay-Bar riders came in to tell about seeing some men up there and from the description he gave, Lamar said one of them had to be your brother. And when you came back so quick after he sent you up—well . . ."

He nodded and gazed off into the distance. Then he said, "I smell you got coffee cooking. You reckon you might spare me a cup?"

She looked puzzled, so he added, "I got some thinking to do and I ain't think so good in the morning without I had no coffee. I'll drink it out here."

Still with the puzzled frown on her face, she turned away. In a moment she came back with a cup of coffee.

Wordlessly, she handed it to him and he seated himself on the step. The dog set his big head on his knee.

He sipped at the coffee; then asked, "Glynn gone up there alone?"

"Yes."

"How long he been gone?"

"He left yesterday morning."

"Their camp's better'n a day's ride, if a man knows where he's going. Only *he* ain't know. Likely he'd go to wherever that Jay-Bar rider seen the men and he'd look for sign to follow." He looked up at her as if he'd asked a question and she nodded in agreement with his speculation.

"Then likely he ain't dead yet," he muttered. "Likely he ain't get himself killed until tomorrow or maybe the next day."

Her face went suddenly white and he realized it was a thought he shouldn't have spoken out loud. Not in front of *her*. He tried suggesting, "Maybe he ain't get killed at all."

It didn't seem to ease her concern. Likely even she could see what the odds were, Clant thought. Glynn had no idea how many men Fairweather had with him or where the lookouts would be posted. He didn't even know where the camp was. Alone, just following sign, he'd likely blunder under one of the guard's guns and be shot off his horse before he could realize what was happening.

It was painful to look at Nora Ellison's expression. It gave Clant thought he'd never considered before. He turned away, busying himself for a moment with the last of the plug of Dan'l Webster. When he looked back at Nora again, he asked, "He mean a lot to you, ain't he?"

She nodded slightly. When she spoke her voice was

99

very small. "He means everything to me. He's everything in the world to me."

"Maybe there's time yet I could fetch him back," Clant said. The words had come without his planning them and the thought startled him. He considered it.

"Will you?" Nora was saying anxiously. "Can you?"

"I ain't know for sure till I try," he answered. He got to his feet and held out the coffee cup to her. She wrapped her fingers around it, but she didn't seem to be aware of it.

"Man ain't know what he can do till he tries, does he?" he added as he bent and jerked open the war bag. "You got a dollar?"

"What?" she asked vaguely.

"A dollar," he repeated as he brought out the gunbelt. He unrolled it and slung it around his waist. Settling the holster in place on his thigh, he drew out the Remington. "This thing ain't throw rocks. And I ain't got money for lead."

Her eyes went to the gun as if it were a rattlesnake. In a voice that was almost a whisper, she asked, "There'll be shooting?"

"Maybe not. Depends where I find this sheriff of your'n." He dropped the revolver back into the holster. The sight of it seemed to have upset her worse. He was sorry it was her he had to ask for the money, but there wasn't anybody else. "You got a dollar?" he said again.

She turned and walked slowly into the kitchen. When she came back it was with a silver dollar in her hand. She held it out hesitantly, and her eyes seemed uncertain.

He wiped his mouth with the back of his hand. She must have a pretty low notion of him, he thought, if she figured he'd steal money off her that way.

"I ain't run away with it," he mumbled as he took the coin from her fingers. "Maybe I ain't come back, but I ain't run away again."

"No, that's not . . . Clant, what I mean is—" she broke off whatever she was trying to say and looked away from him.

He swung the war bag up onto his shoulder and started away; then he stopped and glanced at the dog following at his heels.

"Ma'am," he said, turning back to Nora, "I got to ask a favor off you. I ain't never like to boss Dog here around. He's got his right to come and go where he want. But maybe he ain't better come with me this time. Maybe you got a shed you could close him up in till I've gone so's he won't foller after me."

"I'll take him inside the house," she said softly.

"I ain't think he's housebroke."

"Clant, —" She was close to crying. Dabbing at her eyes with one hand, she took a breath. "I'm sorry. You . . . take care of yourself, Clant."

He remembered that it was the same thing she'd said to Glynn. It seemed strange for her to be saying it to him. And then she was crying, pressing her face into her hands to cover the tears.

It gave him an uncommon feeling of helplessness. He had a strong urge to put his arms around her and try to comfort her. He felt he'd promise her anything in the world that she might want if it would stop her from crying.

What she wanted, he told himself, was Lamar Glynn back alive.

He took a step toward her and stuffed his fingers down into his hip pockets to keep his hands from getting anyplace they didn't belong. Huskily, he said, "Look here now, ma'am, you ain't start worrying yet. You give me three, four days at least. Maybe a week. If I ain't brought him back to you by then, you go ahead and worry all you want. But you ain't start now, you hear?"

She raised her eyes and looked at him over her fingertips.

He grinned hopefully.

She moved her hands away from her face. Nodding, she smiled. It was a very small smile, but she was trying.

The stable was closer so he picked up his horse first and asked a few questions about the mount Glynn had ridden. Then he headed for Langer's mercantile.

Stores had always intrigued him and this was a particularly interesting one, a big barn of a place with its rafters hung with pots and pans and copper-bottomed boilers that gleamed dully. The shelves, loaded with coffee mills and coal-oil lamps and goods in brightly colored wrappers, seemed as if they must hold just about everything made by man. There were harnesses with brass buckles, new rifles and handguns that almost begged to be used, and bins filled with foodstuffs. The whole place smelled of oil and leather and spices.

As he walked in, Clant paused and took a deep breath. Across the store, he saw Langer busily showing bolt goods to a large woman in a lavish flowered bonnet. The shopkeeper gave him a quick look and went on spreading cloth out for the woman. He didn't seem likely to be finished with her soon.

Clant hoisted himself over the counter and started pulling down the airtights he wanted from the stacks on the shelves. He set them on the counter; then he picked up a box of cartridges for the Spencer and took a handful. As he put the box back, he glanced at the powder and shot. But this time it might be important how quickly he could reload the handgun, so he turned to hunt for cartridges.

By the time he'd located a box of Colt's Combustible Envelope Cartridges, Calibre 44, and started counting out what he wanted, Langer had deserted the large woman and was scurrying anxiously across the store toward him.

"What do you want?" the little man bellowed as he hurried around the end of the counter.

Clant put down the cartridges and set the box back on the shelf. "Small box of caps," he muttered, scanning the shelves.

Langer grabbed down a box of Americans and slapped it on the counter.

"No," Clant said. "I want Eley's."

"You generally buy the cheapest."

"I generally ain't too particular if they fire or not." Clant spotted the box he wanted and set it down next to the cartridges. "Eley's is the best and even them, a man can figure one in a dozen ain't gonna fire for him. Them is long enough odds to satisfy me. You figure that up."

"Got cash money?"

He flipped the silver dollar down on the counter.

"You already owe me—"

"You see me payday for what I already owe you. This here is for this stuff."

Langer hesitated. Then he picked up a pencil. With a wave of his hands he shooed Clant back to the other side of the counter; then he began, making notations on a ruled pad by the cash register.

Setting his two-bit piece down on top of the cartwheel, Clant said, "Give me my change in Dan'l

Webster."

Langer glanced at the money and grunted. Then he put a total under the figures and added the tobacco to the stack of goods.

Clant pulled the pad toward himself and turned it around. Langer watched impatiently as he studied it, tapping his thumb across his fingers as he counted. Looking up, Clant said, "You gonna wrap them goods for me, or you want I should use 'em up here?"

The shopkeeper snorted through his nose as he turned away to find a piece of used wrapping paper. And Clant leaned across the counter.

When Langer turned back again to spread the paper and pile the goods on it, Clant had another plug of tobacco stuffed into his off pocket and was again pretending to struggle with the figures on the pad. When he felt he'd wasted enough of Langer's time he nodded with satisfaction, picked up the bundle by the cord, and walked out. Behind him, he could hear the storekeeper muttering irritated apologies to the large woman as he rushed back to spread more bolt goods.

CHAPTER 9

CLANT LOCATED THE SHERIFF'S TRAIL MORE EASILY than he expected. He'd never counted himself an expert tracker, but the rain-soaked earth of the game trails took prints clean and clear and Glynn's horse had left distinctive marks. It had been freshly shod behind. The prints of the new shoes paired with the marks of the frogs and trimmed horn of the unshod forehooves, were as easy to follow as blazed trees.

The way he read it, the sheriff had covered ground

fast and had cut sign early in his hunt. Marks of the new shoes topped over older prints of other horses and headed directly up toward the Rocks. He followed as long as there was light and on into the darkness. But eventually the night cold and the clouds that scudded over the face of the moon caused him to bed down. Hunting alone in the night, without even Dog as company, was a thing he didn't much fancy. And shadowed in the skittering moonlight, he likely wouldn't get far with it. He did without a fire, eating cold beans from a can, and then wrapped himself in the horse blanket.

It was still cold come morning, and frost lay over the trail. But he knew where he was heading and it was easy enough picking out Glynn's sign along the way. The prints kept going straight up toward the outlaw camp. On toward midmorning, though, after the sun had raised the frost, the trail went sour.

Halting, he swung down off the dun horse to study the ground. He was close under the shadow of one of Fairweather's guard posts and that, in itself, worried him. Studying the churned earth underfoot, he decided Glynn's horse had reared, wheeled, and bolted into the grass. Because Glynn had seen something that sent him off the trail? Or because the horse had been spooked, maybe by a gunshot?

He picked up a stone about the size of his fist and gazed at the small, dark stain on it. Dried blood?

Jerking up his head at the trill of a solitaire, he answered with a hooting whistle. When the same shrill hoot came back to him, he rose and faced up toward the man who appeared atop the high rocks.

"You could get yourself killed," the man called.

He called back, "Had trouble down here?" When the

105

guard nodded in reply, he asked, "What happened?"

"Snooper. Got him though."

With a miserable empty feeling in his stomach, Clant stepped up onto the dun and headed uptrail, toward the camp. It wouldn't be easy to take that news back to Nora Ellison.

When he rode into the camp, Fairweather and Isham came to meet him. It was Fairweather who asked, "What brings you back up here? Trouble in town?"

"Yeah," he said as he stepped down off the horse.

Isham looked him down and said darkly, "You're wearing a gun."

"Yeah."

"I heard you ain't wear a gun no more."

"I got it on me now."

"What happened in town?" Fairweather asked. "They wise to us or did you get yourself into trouble?"

Clant shrugged and headed toward the fire. "Sheriff down there ain't take too kindly a man gets friendly with his woman," he said as they followed along after him. He looked into the pot. More beans.

"You reckon you're full-growed now, ain't you, boy?" Ish grunted.

"When'd all this happen?" Fairweather asked.

"I ain't recall. Couple or three days ago."

"Where you been since then?" That was Ish, sounding vaguely suspicious.

"Riding around."

Fairweather grinned. "Running from that sheriff? Well, you got no reason to worry about him no more."

"Why not?" Clant asked.

"Rufe shot him down yesterday."

"How'd that happen?"

"He stuck his nose up the trail back a ways and Rufe

106

put a couple of Winchester slugs into him. You ain't got any more worries about him now."

"What's the matter, boy?" Ish said. "You ain't look none too happy. Got somebody else chasing you too?"

"Not as I know of." Clant scooped himself up a bait of beans and took a mouthful.

Isham spread a grin on his face. Heartily, he said, "Well, you ain't concern yourself now, boy. You just rest easy and make yourself to home. Enjoy them vittles and we'll talk about it later." He gave Fairweather a nudge and the two drifted away together.

Clant stood watching them as he ate. It didn't seem right, he thought. Isham should have given him hell for messing things up in town and for letting Glynn get that close to the camp. Maybe since the sheriff was dead anyways, Ish didn't care. But that wasn't his way. He should care that his orders hadn't been followed, shouldn't he?

Still puzzled by his brother's behavior, he finished off the beans and began to drift around the camp. He knew he wasn't particularly welcome among the men, and without even Dog at his heels, he felt damnably alone.

Somebody'd brought in a deer and he found Lady hacking steaks off it. She gave him a sincere welcome and he spent most of the afternoon helping her and running over his own thoughts. But he didn't come up with any answers. One fact stood: Glynn was dead.

He had to take that news back to Nora Ellison, no matter how much he might hate the chore. He couldn't answer himself *why* he had to go through with it, but he knew that he had to. And he couldn't give himself a good reason why he felt so damn disturbed by the sheriff's death.

It was nearly twilight when they finished stringing the

steaks on sharp poles and hanging them over the fire. The woodsmoke smelled good and the fire gave off a fair warmth, but there was a biting cold wind blowing down through the rocks, and he decided it was time to dig the short coat out of his war bag. When he got back with it on, Lady was gone from the fire, but Ish and Paul and some of the boys had gathered there.

As Clant walked up, Ish looked at the coat. He hunkered down and filled a cup with coffee. Rising, he held it out and said, "Here, boy, this'll warm you a mite."

Clant reached for the cup and suddenly Isham's hand jerked. Clant winced, stumbling back as the hot coffee was flung into his face. At the same time he felt his arms being grabbed from behind. More than one man had hold of him, and one of them was getting a rope on his wrists.

He shouted, trying to struggle free, but they had a good hold on him. As the knots were jerked tight, they threw their weight on him, forcing him down on his knees.

Brother Isham watched and grinned as one of the men got the loose end of the rope around Clant's ankles and snugged it.

Clant fought against the rope but it was tied firm. He was on his knees and helpless. If he kept struggling about all he'd succeed in doing would be throwing himself flat on the ground like a pigged calf. That would make things even worse. His eyes stung from the coffee and the wind had already begun to chill his wet face and clothes. Blinking, he looked up at Isham and shouted, "What the hell is this all about?"

"Boy, I just plain ain't trust you," Ish answered, still grinning. "You're a sneaking, low-down, useless, shiftless, no-good, lying little snake. Ain't nobody trust you, 'specially not your own family what knows you best. You ain't no good. You never was and you never will be. We got us big plans, Paul and me, and we ain't. give you no chance to ruin 'em for us."

"What the hell I do this time?" Clant protested.

Isham shrugged. "Maybe nothing. Maybe you been telling us true about this town of Jubilee and this sheriff and this deputy job he give you. But maybe you ain't. Right, Paul?"

Fairweather nodded in agreement.

"Maybe you have throwed in with the law. You change color too quick to suit me, Little Brother. Sometime I tell you to do something, you fight me. Sometime you take my orders without you argue none at all. One day you ain't wear a gun no more and you ain't want in with us. 'Nother day you ride up here with iron on your hip. I ain't like it none. And I ain't like you none. So I ain't take no chance with you. I know you too good to trust you, brother Clant." Ish glanced toward Fairweather again.

"Yeah," the outlaw agreed. "Feller gets as spooky about going back to prison as Clant here, there's no telling what he might do or who he might throw in with."

Isham hunkered down and unbuckled Clant's gunbelt. He jerked it from around his waist and pulled the revolver out of the holster.

"Ain't a bad gun," he said, hefting it. "Ain't hold a candle to these new model Colts, though. You tried one of these new model Colts, boy?" When he got no answer, he raised the gun as if to swing it down into Clant's face and repeated his question.

"Yeah," Clant muttered.

109

"Surprised you never got yourself one," Ish said. "The way you always figured you was king of the hill when you had a gun in your hand. I'll tell you something, Little Brother. A gun ain't enough to make a man out'n a damn snot-nosed brat. It wasn't then and it ain't now." He turned the Remington in his hands, studying it by the light of the fire. Thoughtfully, he said, "Y'know, boy, I just might take this here gun with me when we ride into town. Might be I'll drop it there. Anybody down to that town know your gun, boy? Might be I'll ride that dun horse of your'n, too. Anybody know that horse of your'n by sight, boy? Be funny, wouldn't it, if somebody got the notion you was riding along with us? Be real funny if you was to get sent back. 'Specially if it was for something you *didn't* do."

He was still chuckling over the thought as he moved around behind Clant and helped himself to the sheath knife. He sent it flying over Clant's shoulder. It hit the ground point-first and buried itself up to the hilt.

"Nice balance," he muttered; then he called to the men watching, "Gimme a hand with him."

Two of them grabbed Clant by the shoulders and dragged him away from the fire. They left him on his knees under the overhang of the cliff.

He sat back on his heels trying to ease his tense muscles and thankful that, at least, Isham hadn't left him flat on his face. He felt damn well miserable enough the way he was. The rocky ground had slashed at his knees as he was dragged. His legs had begun to cramp and the rope between his wrists and ankles was snubbed too tight for him to shift position at all.

Isham wasn't likely to let him up soon either, he figured. Brother Isham was concerned with learning him his place and it was likely to be a long and painful

110

lesson.

He asked himself if maybe he shouldn't learn quick. Maybe he should give in first chance Ish gave him. Ish sure planned to be certain he got identified as one of the robbers after they hit the Jubilee bank. He'd be outlawed again and that would be that. Sure as hell nobody'd believe his story and, like Glynn had warned, wasn't any judge going to go easy on him the next time. Once he got the outlaw brand on him again, it wasn't going to come off. Brother Isham would own him.

He shivered at the wind that swept along the face of the cliff. There was ice in it, and a hint of coming snow.

Someone was coming toward him. He opened his eyes and lifted his chin up off his chest. It was Lady, her white dress ghostly in the moonlight. She had a plate in one hand and a cup in the other.

"You asleep, Clant?" she asked softly.

"No," he said. "I ache too much to sleep."

"You hungry?" she held out the plate.

"No."

"I brung you supper. And coffee."

"I ain't want any," he mumbled.

She sounded disappointed, "Ain't nothing you want?"

"Sure. Loose my hands."

"Clant, you know I can't do that. Paul would peel the skin right off me if I was to set you loose."

"Yeah," he said between his teeth.

She stood there, holding the food and looking at him. "Ain't there nothing else?" she asked sadly.

"If you ain't help me get loose, maybe you'll reach in my pocket and give me a chaw?"

She set down the dishes and knelt in front of him. "They gonna kill you, Clant?" she asked as she dug out the plug and held it up for him.

He bit off a good-sized chunk and worked it a couple of times before he answered her. "Ain't likely. He'll just tie me up so good I can't move but what way he leads me."

"He got you tied up pretty good now," she said as she shoved the plug back into his pocket.

"You turn my collar up for me?" he asked.

As she did it, she said, "Clant, you mind I set with you a while?"

"Hell, no. I could use a mite of company."

She spread her skirts and seated herself on the ground. Then she picked up the dish and began hacking at the steak. Clant gazed thoughtfully at the knife she used. "Wouldn't be nothing to it," he said.

"To what?"

"You just give a little cut to this here rope they got on me. Then you fetch yourself back over to the fire. I'd set here real still till they was bedded and they'd never know how I got loose."

"No," she answered, shaking her head. "Paul would figure it out. He's real smart. He'd sure skin me."

"Lady, if I ain't get loose, Brother Ish is gonna skin me."

She fell silent as she nibbled at a piece of the meat. Then she said, "You ought to eat something, Clant. You gotta keep your strength up." She stabbed a piece of the venison and held it out toward him.

He spat tobacco juice and then took the meat off the point of the knife with his teeth. When he'd swallowed, she held the coffee cup for him. He drank and then said, "Like Dog."

"What?"

"That old hound that follers me," he told her. "I feed

112

him off the end of a knife like that. It don't make him no mind on account he ain't got hands in the first place. Man, though, it hurts his pride he get himself so hog-tied he can't even feed himself. Hurts his pride he get himself so cornered he can't do but what he gets told to do."

She sat back silently as if she had some thought of her own she was studying. Then she said in a small voice, "A lady's got herself pride too, Clant. It hurts her to be give away like she was just an ol' shirt or a horse or something." She stabbed at a piece of meat as if it were something alive that she meant to kill.

"What you mean?" he asked.

It took her a minute to work up to saying it. "Paul don't want me no more. He done went and give me away. To that damned ol' brother of your'n. I don't like him, Clant. He ain't no gentleman *no* which way."

He looked at her, at the pale thin face that looked like silver in the moonlight. So Isham owned her now, too. The thought of that added to his misery.

She offered him the piece of meat but he shook his head and she ate it herself, taking her time chewing it, as if she were deep in thought.

The night wind gusted along the cliff face and she shivered. With a toss of her head, she said, "It gets right cold up here. Back home, to the big house, it never got so cold. And when it did we all had pretty coats to put on us when we went to ride in the buggy."

"You can have my coat if you'll take it off me," he said. But she didn't seem to hear him. She was looking past him.

He turned his head and saw what she was staring at. The figure looming toward them was Isham. He stepped up in front of Clant and rested his knuckles on his hips.

113

"Boy, what are you doing with my woman?" he said.

"What you think?" Clant snapped back at him. "Like this, I ain't do much but talk to her."

"Little Brother, you ain't even *talk* to nobody without you get leave from me, you hear?" Ish grabbed Lady by the shoulder and jerked her to her feet. She squealed in pain at the grip of his hand and dropped the plate.

"You stay 'way from him," he told her. "You stay 'way from everybody but me, you hear? 'Specially, you stay 'way from him."

She nodded and he gave her a shove toward the fire. "You get on over. Clear up the wreck and then fetch yourself to my sugans, you hear?"

She walked away slowly, with her head hung down.

Isham turned back to Clant. "You gonna sass me again, boy?"

"Likely."

Ish swung hard, open-handed, slapping him in the face, almost knocking him over. "You gonna sass me again, boy?" he repeated.

Clant nodded.

Isham hit him again. "What you say?"

What was the use? Clant answered, "No, I ain't sass you again."

" 'Nother thing, from now on you gonna say *sir* when you talk to me. You hear, boy?"

"Yessir."

"You study on that a while, boy," Ish said, grinning. "I'll see can you recall it come morning." He turned and walked away.

Watching him, Clant drew a deep breath and let it out with a sigh. Someday brother Isham was gonna make one damn big mistake. Someday brother Isham was gonna let him get his good hand on a gun again.

CHAPTER 10

THE NIGHT GUARDS HAD GONE OUT AND THE DAY guards had come in. The fire was banked and the camp fell silent except for snores and occasional grunts. The moon moved across the sky so slowly that it seemed to Clant that day should have come and gone and come again, and yet it wasn't even full overhead. Its light gave the heavy frost that lay on the ground the look of fresh-cut silver. And the wind ate into his bones.

He'd told Lady true. He ached too damn much to sleep. He'd closed his eyes and tucked his chin down to shield his face as best he could from the wind. His thoughts blurred with the weariness he felt. But he couldn't sleep.

The wind came in gusts, howling through the rocks like the voices of the dead and darkening the moon with thick scuds of clouds. Something wailed.

It might have been just the wind in a crevice or a tree. But it sounded god-awful like a screech owl. Screech owls didn't range up here, he told himself. But the sound of it shivered down his spine. A screech owl howling was a sure sign of death.

It wasn't the thought of death that bothered him. Death was a common enough thing and dying was something a man knew he'd sooner or later have to face up to. But the way an owl could know beforehand and the mournful voice it gave to its prophecy was a fearsome thing. Was it only the wind that moaned in the night, or did the dead really come back to plague the living? Was it them as had died hard who came to haunt the ones that killed them? Or was it them as had lived hard who had to walk the burying grounds at night? Or was it only the varmints and the wind? And when a man was dead, was that the end of him?

How did the screech owl know before the time come that someone was sure to die?

Clant tensed suddenly. Something had moved and he was damn sure it wasn't the wind. He heard the soft, whispery sound again and looked up. Something was coming toward him, something pale and wispy like a haunt in its winding sheet. He felt his heart jump in his chest. And then he grinned at his own fool thoughts.

It was Lady, her white dress catching the moonlight, rustling in the wind. She came up quietly and stopped in front of him.

He tried to swallow but his mouth was dust-dry. "Gimme a chaw, Lady," he said to her, his voice dry too, and barely a whisper.

She dropped to her knees and dug into his pocket for the plug. It wasn't until he'd bit off a piece and she'd put the plug back that she spoke.

"Clant, I won't stay here no more," she said hoarsely. He could tell from her voice that she'd been crying. She was still close to it. "Not with that no-good brother of your'n."

"He hurt you?" he asked her.

She nodded. "Clant, if'n I let you loose, will you take me with you?" Reaching into the front of her dress, she pulled out a knife.

"Cut me loose," he said intensely.

"You gotta promise me you'll take me with you."

"You cut me loose, I promise anything you want."

She moved around behind him and as she began sawing at the rope she said, "You're lying to me, Clant Meldrin."

The rope gave and his hands came free. His arms shot

116

with pain as he tried to move them. He managed to get his hands around in front of him and rubbed his numb fingers together as Lady hacked at the rope on his ankles. When he felt it give he tried to shift his legs. He was able to move a bit but he couldn't stand up. He'd have to sit a minute till the pain of the cramped muscles eased.

He felt Lady slip the knife into the sheath on his belt and then she came around in front of him again. She took hold of his hand and began to rub his wrist where the rope had dug into it. He leaned his back against the rock and looked at her.

"If you think I was lying, how come you let me loose?" he asked.

"I don't hold it again' you, Clant," she said softly, and he could hear how close she was to crying. "But we gotta get away from him. Both of us got to. If'n I left you, he'd do you real mean."

He nodded and tried moving his arm. It was still painful and the movement was jerky, but at least he could do it. Bracing himself, he struggled to his feet. "Come on," he said, taking hold of her outstretched hand, "and keep quiet."

The first steps were awkward and painful, but as his blood began to flow freely through his veins, moving got easier. He led the girl along the face of the cliff to the foot of the rocks where they'd climbed and she'd sung to him. That way they could cross behind the guard on the trail. He gave her a boost and she scrambled up; then she offered a hand down to help him follow.

With a gesture, he shooed her on ahead and hauled himself up after her. Catching up, he led her along in the shadows of the rocks until they were well away from the camp.

"You want to rest a minute?" he asked, still whispering against the silence of the night.

She nodded and seated herself against a rock.

He dropped down by her side. He'd had to stop and rest himself. His body still ached from the ropes.

She leaned up against him, resting her head on his shoulder, and he could feel her shiver. Slipping an arm around her, he asked, "Ain't you got no coat?"

"I had to get away from *him*," she said. "I was afeared to try to get it. But I ain't cold."

"Sure, you ain't. I ain't neither." He pulled off the short coat and put it over her shoulders.

"You're a gentleman, Clant," she said as she slipped her arms into the sleeves. "You won't leave me here, will you?"

"No," he told her.

"I did bring something." She worked her hand down into the folds of her skirts. "Only I was afeared if I give it to you, you'd take it and leave me." She brought out her hand. There was a gun in it. "It's your'n, ain't it?"

He wrapped his fingers around the butt of the Remington and it settled snug and secure into his hand. Grinning, he said, "Lady, I love you."

She eased her head back against her shoulder. "You're lying to me, Clant Meldrin. But it's a nice lie."

"Where you want me to take you?" he asked. As the wind whipped the clouds away from the face of the moon he checked over the gun. It was still loaded. Six cartridges and six caps.

"Anywhere," her voice was soft and sleepy. "Wherever you're going."

He thought about that and answered, "I ain't been going nowhere. I just been running from where I was. I

118

ain't know where to go."

"Anywhere," she murmured; and he realized that she was almost asleep.

He couldn't let her sleep. They had to get moving again. With luck no one would find they'd gotten away till dawn woke the camp. But he couldn't trust to luck. If Isham were to catch up with them—well, Isham had a damned strong and unforgiving pride. He sure wouldn't much like his little brother running off with his woman.

He shook her shoulder, "Come on, Lady. We got to cover ground."

She raised her head, "Where we going?"

"Right now for a long walk. I ain't dare take a chance on trying to steal horses from under Fairweather's guard. We'll do better if we try to keep hid than if we wake them up and try to outrun 'em."

"Where we gonna walk to?" she asked sleepily as he led her into the maze of boulders and outcropping rocks.

"Town of Jubilee. I got something I got to tend to in Jubilee first. After that, I'll take you wherever you want."

The rocks sloped down into a meadow, white with frost under the bright moon. Before they reached it, Clant caught her hand again and halted her in the shadows.

Catching her breath, she asked him, "What you got to do in Jubilee?"

"I come up here to look for that sheriff. Now I got to go tell his woman he's dead."

"That the feller what Rufus shot down yesterday? He ain't dead. Leastways he wasn't yesterday."

"What?" Clant grabbed her arm. "What you mean, Lady?"

"I was up on top the rocks taking the air and I seen it

119

all. I seen more'n that ol' Rufus did. Rufe put a bullet in him and his horse run off toward the cliff down yonder." She pointed down, across the meadow. "Then Rufe got a bullet into the horse and it went right off the cliff. Only that sheriff, he didn't. He got himself off the ol' horse and down into the tall grass. After a while, he crawled off up into them far rocks, dragging himself like he was hurt. But he sure weren't dead. And that Rufe, he's just too damn lazy to even go look, make sure what he shot."

"He weren't dead," Clant muttered after her. "Lady, you reckon you could find for me where you seen him go?"

"I reckon. What you want to go there for?"

He fingered the plug out of his pocket and bit off a chunk. Then he answered her. "If Glynn's still alive, I 'spose I'm gonna have to fetch *him* back down to Jubilee too."

"Why?"

He considered a moment. "Damn if I know. But I gotta do it."

"All right," she said. "You come on. I'll show you where I seen him." She started along in the shadows. Suddenly she jerked, turning toward him and gasping. There was an arm locked around her throat and the muzzle of a gun thrust from under her arm.

"Drop that revolver, brother Clant," Isham said, holding the girl in front of him as if she were a shield as he leveled his Colt at Clant.

There was no chance for a shot. Isham was too well protected behind Lady. Clant let the gun slip out of his fingers. It clattered on the stony ground. Slowly, he raised his hands.

Isham pushed the girl aside, flinging her to the

120

ground. He grinned and the moonlight made devil-shadows of his face as he said, "Ain't you never learn nothing, boy?"

"No," Clant answered him.

"That's the pure gospel truth. You set me in mind of a stud-horse I had me once, boy. You recall him—black colt what wouldn't never settle down under a saddle. I tried nigh onto every way they is to tame him. You recall, boy?"

Clant nodded slightly.

"You recall how I finally had to learn him to behave himself, boy?" When he got no answer, Isham demanded again, "You recall, boy?"

"Yeah. I recall."

"Damn shame, weren't it? He was a good horse, with good blood. Only good blood ain't always breed true." Ish grinned, "I couldn't tame him no other way. But I took the knife to him, that settled him down. You reckon I'm gonna have to learn you the same way, boy?"

Clant shifted the quid and said, "You try take a knife to me, you damn well better mean to kill me with it."

He saw Lady move. She was reaching for the gun he'd dropped. But Isham saw it too.

Still grinning, Ish turned the Colt toward her. The hammer was already back and he began to close his finger on the trigger.

Clant let fly the wad of tobacco juice at his face and jumped. The gun went off in Isham's hand, slamming lead into the ground. Ish swabbed at his eyes with one hand, the other thumbing at the hammer of the Colt. But Clant's fist rammed him hard in the gut.

He stumbled back, still trying to get the Colt cocked, and Clant caught him well under the belt buckle with

121

one boot.

Ish doubled over, grunting in pain. Clant's other fist came up under his jaw and he went backwards, tumbling down the slope.

Lady had the revolver in her hand. As Clant grabbed it from her, she rose and brushed at her skirts. "He ain't no gentleman at all!"

Glancing at the figure of his brother stirring in the moonlight, Clant muttered, "He ain't dead neither. Come on!" He wrapped a hand around her wrist and started her running, down out of the rocks and straight across the frosted grass, heedless of cover now. There were more rocks and clumps of trees across the meadow. But it was a damn long run.

He winced at the sound of a rifle, but wherever the slug went, it wasn't close. From somewhere behind he heard the night guard sing out.

"Isham!" the man called, "You need help?"

And he heard his brother shout back in a voice that was sharp with pain and anger, "Goddammit, no! You stay put! He's *my* kin and *I'll* settle for him!"

Clant grinned a bit at that. A man could make himself trouble by having too much pride. As they reached the rocks he pulled Lady down into cover and dropped to his knees beside her. She grabbed at his arm. "Clant, I'm scared!"

"Why? It ain't only but Isham chasing us," he said, scanning the meadow for sign of Ish following. He could see nothing. Feeling the fear in Lady's touch, he told her, "Ain't much cause to be feared of Ish by himself. Not now."

"He's got a gun—"

"Sure, but we got one, too. And I got a damn sight better hand with it than him."

"You sure, Clant?"

"Hell, I know Ish. He ain't much for steadying up his gun nor taking care where he shoots. 'Specially not when he's all excited, way he is now. He just throws a mess of lead and hopes he hits something. Ain't likely he's gonna hit nothing he ain't right on top of." He hoped he sounded more certain than he felt. Tugging at her hand, he added, "You come on along, real slow now. Keep to cover and don't make no noise."

He led her through the shadows, moving cautiously. The problem was to lose Ish if they could. And if they couldn't—well—Clant figured that he would face up to that problem if it came to face him.

"Yonder," Lady whispered suddenly, startling him. "That's where your ol' sheriff went to." She stretched out her arm and pointed toward an uprising of weathered rock across a frost-white clearing.

Clant halted and looked out over the ground. There was some brush in the little meadow and there were a few scattered rocks big enough to offer cover. But from one to another would be a run over the open grass.

He glanced up at the sky. Clouds scudded across the face of the moon, but there was still enough light to set off anything that moved against the open ground. And it would be a while yet before the damn moon set.

Holding Lady with a gesture, he listened to the sounds around them. Varmints and a lot of wind. Too much wind. It came in ragged gusts and all around them the dry grass rustled and the shedding trees groaned, their branches cracking as they rubbed together. If it was a man and not an animal or the wind that made any of the noises he heard, he couldn't tell it.

He wrapped his free hand around hers again and said, "Come on." Together they ran over the field toward the cover of a mass of rock.

There were three shots, all of them thrown too fast and from too far away, but Clant winced at the sound and threw himself toward the shadows, dragging Lady with him. As they went down onto the ground behind the rock, she flung her arm around his neck.

"I'm scared," she whimpered.

"Ain't no cause," he told her again as he pulled her head down onto his right shoulder, keeping his gun hand clear of her. From the way she trembled and drew her breath, he was afraid she was about to cry. "Ain't you trust me?" he asked.

She caught her breath and he felt her head nod against his chest. She was trying to trust him but she couldn't—not quite. Why the hell not? he thought angrily. Then he answered himself—what reason did she have to trust him? She already knew him too well.

"You sit here and stay still," he told her. "I'm gonna find out just where he is."

He crept to the edge of the shadow. He had a pretty good idea of where Isham had been when he'd fired. Gathering a handful of pebbles, he flung them.

He drew fire. He saw the blossom of flame from Isham's gun and muttered to himself, "Pap would strap you good, brother Isham, you let yourself get possumed like that."

Ish was closer now. He'd moved in after them and was well within range of the Colt. And within range of Clant's Remington, too.

Listening for some sound of Ish moving, Clant leveled the revolver, bracing it against the rock. Six cartridges and six caps, he thought to himself, and maybe there wasn't a dud in the lot. Maybe.

Right-handed, he scooped up more pebbles and sent

124

them skittering across the grass.

The Colt flashed and Clant had his sights on it. He knew the Remington from long practice, knew it as if it were a part of himself. And now he had his target spotted. His finger closed on the trigger. He felt the hammer release into its long, slow arc.

He felt his hand tremble. Even as the hammer struck, even as the cap exploded under it, he knew it was a bad shot. And he knew why.

He rubbed the back of his free hand across his face. It was damp with sweat. His mouth was dry and his teeth were dug into his lower lip. Angrily, he dropped back into the shadow, next to Lady, and dug into his pocket for the tobacco.

"You get him?" she asked eagerly.

"No!" He snapped the word at her so hard that she drew back from him.

Tensely, she waited.

After a moment, he spoke, his voice calmer now, "I ain't smart, Lady. I pulled six shots off him and now I been sitting here, letting him load up again."

"Clant," she said, reaching out and touching his arm. "What we gonna do now?"

He spat and then answered her. "I'm going over to where you seen that sheriff get off to. I want you to stay put here and watch where I go to. I'm gonna pull Isham's fire again. You count his shots. Minute he's fired off six, you run like hell for where you seen me go. You hear?" If she nodded, he couldn't see it. He asked again, "You hear?"

"Yes," she said softly. "Clant, mind out."

"Sure," he muttered. He spat again and crouched at the edge of the shadow, waiting. The rags of wind-blown clouds were whirling over the face of the moon.

As it darkened, he ran. Head down, with the revolver cradled against his chest, he dashed for the cover of the shadows across the grass.

The moon came free of its clouds and caught him, stretching out a long shadow behind him. And he heard Isham's shots. Again, three, but thrown more carefully this time. He was aware of a slug cutting into the grass behind him. Isham was well within the gun's range now, and calmer. But he was still rushing, guessing instead of leading his target.

And Clant was on the edge of cover. He threw himself down behind a massive outcrop of rock. Crouching, he moved toward the side of it. He had to force Isham into three more shots before Lady could move safely. But he had to take care. Once Ish calmed enough to start really using his sights, he'd be damned dangerous. Would the pebble trick work again?

As he reached down to gather a handful of loose stones he heard a fourth gunshot. A slug slammed into the rock, close enough to send a spray of chips against the back of his neck.

He wheeled, pressing his shoulders against the rock. That shot had come from behind him.

He saw the flash of the gun as it fired again and he felt the nearness of the slug. Whoever was behind that gun was plenty close enough, but lost in the utter pitch blackness under the overhang of rock. He was too damn close to miss, Clant thought. He hugged his back to the rock, knowing that the moonlight on the frost-covered grass behind him would silhouette him to the man with the gun.

He had a notion he knew who it was holding that gun. He called out in a loud whisper, "Glynn?"

He thought he could hear the gun hammer cock.

"Glynn! It's me, Clant Meldrin!"

The slug jerked at his vest as the gun flashed again.

"Goddammit, leave off with killing me for a minute!" he shouted hoarsely as he lunged into the darkness. He threw himself down and under the gun, sweeping out with right hand.

He judged well. His wrist struck the barrel of the revolver. He grabbed, his fingers wrapping around the cylinder. There was fight in the hand that held it, but it was weak and he was able to jerk the gun free of it.

"Glynn?" he said again. He couldn't see at all in this dark shadow, but he could hear the shallow-drawn breathing. Stuffing the Remington into his waistband, he got himself up onto one knee and reached out. His hand found the man's shoulder and he asked, "Glynn, you hurt?"

The sheriff spoke, his voice coming hard. "Are you riding with Fairweather again, Clant?"

"No. That woman of your'n sent me up here to fetch you home. You hurt bad?"

"Leg's busted."

Clant ran his fingers over the gun he'd wrenched out of the sheriff's hand. It was one of the new model Colt revolvers, same kind as Isham had. He asked, "You got cartridges for this gun?"

"Yeah. In my belt."

He located the sheriff's gunbelt with his fingers and jerked it free. He swung it around his own waist, twisting the buckle to the back so that the holster hung under his left hand. Then he stuffed the Remington into it. It was the gun he knew, the one he wanted if things got tight.

Running his hand along the belt, he judged the sheriff to have maybe twenty-five, thirty rounds. He grinned to

127

himself, filled with a sudden sense of wealth. He could afford to waste shots with the Colt. Opening the loading gate, he replaced the rounds Glynn had fired. Damned handy, these self-exploding cartridges. He wished to hell he'd handled this particular weapon before and had some idea of its eccentricities.

"I'll be back," he muttered to the sheriff as he headed toward the meadow. He halted at the edge of the rock, looking across the field. It had began to snow, a light swirling mist of snow blown on the wind. He wiped his face with the back of his hand and leveled the Colt, in the general direction in which he'd last seen Isham's fire. Gently, he drew the hammer back to full cock. The gun sure set well in a man's hand.

He inched himself past the edge of the rock. He fired twice, letting the blaze of the gun spot him for Isham. For an instant after the second shot, he waited with the moonlight on his shoulder, holding the breath he'd caught in his lungs. Then he flung himself back behind cover, his heart pounding against his ribs.

Isham spent the three cartridges Clant had figured him to have left in the gun. He was using the sight now, and he chipped rock close enough to send a shudder along Clant's spine.

As the blaze of the third shot flared out, Clant hollered, "Lady!"

Nothing happened.

He saw no sign of her. He called out again. With his thumb moving across his fingers, he counted, trying to estimate how long it would take Isham to get fresh loads into the gun. The damn new Colts loaded a fair bit faster than a cap-and-ball revolver. Where the hell was she?

He saw her start from the shadows like a frightened rabbit. She had her skirts gathered in her hands and her

128

head tacked down against the sting of the snow that was whipped in the wind. Her skinny legs flashed as she ran and then, suddenly, she was down in the grass. She'd stumbled, and fallen.

Ducking low, with his thumb on the hammer of the Colt, Clant ran toward her. She didn't seem to be moving. He snapped a shot toward Isham, hoping it would distract him and slow him in his reloading.

He saw Lady stir. She raised her head, propping herself on her hands as he reached toward her.

Isham fired two shots. Likely that was all he'd had time to ram into the cylinder, Clant thought as he scooped Lady into his arms. He wheeled back toward the rocks, and she slid her arms around his neck, clinging to him as he ran. He lunged into the darkness where Glynn lay hidden and dropped to his knees. Lady clung to him and he could feel the pounding of her heart.

"You ain't still scared?" he said to her.

"No. I ain't scared no more," she whispered. Something about the sound of her voice, the way she'd said it, seemed wrong.

"Lady, what's the matter?"

She answered plain and simple, with no fear in her voice, "I'm shot, Clant. I think I'm dying."

"Oh, God, no!"

"Hold me."

He let the Colt slip out of his fingers and flattened his hand against her back. "Lady, you ain't die. Please."

He could hear it, though, in her breathing and the rattling in her chest, like she'd taken a ball through the lung and was trying to draw breath through her own blood.

"Clant," she said, the words coming hard to her.

129

"Back home there was a church. Prettiest little ol' white cla'board church you ever want to see. Bell in the tower rang out, you could hear it way back into the swamp." She gagged and coughed.

He held her close, feeling the warm dampness of blood under the hand against her back. "Lady," he whispered.

"Up back of the church was ol' graveyard, all full of oak trees with moss hangin' down like gray beads." She had no voice left. The words were a rustling of the wind. "And 'zaleas. Come spring they was the prettiest things. You ever seen a mess of 'zaleas all full of flowers, Clant?"

He nodded. Her forehead was against his cheek and he could feel the wispy softness of her hair on his face.

"Don't pile no rocks on me, Clant. A churchyard, with a proper hearse and black horses with plumes. It ain't no proper thing . . ." For a moment her words stopped and he thought the breathing had stopped, too. But then she found the strength. "Ain't no proper thing a lady get rocks piled on her in some ol' gully. Please, Clant, promise me. A churchyard."

"I promise it, Lady."

"You tell me true, Clant?"

"Yes, ma'am. I ain't break my word to you, Lady." He hoped she believed him. Just this once, let her believe him!

For a long moment he could still feel the beating of her heart, slow and uneven. And he could hear the sound of her breathing. Then she said, "You're a gentleman, Clant. Only gentleman I ever knowed." It was the last thing she said.

He held her, even when he couldn't feel the beat of her heart any longer and her head leaned limp on his shoulder.

130

Then he eased her down onto the ground. He found her face with his fingertips and touched it lightly. Her eyes were closed. He started a hand for his pocket and then remembered. He didn't have two pennies for her.

CHAPTER 11

"CLANT?" IT WAS GLYNN'S VOICE AND IT STARTLED him. Thoughts of the sheriff had gone out of his mind. He jerked up his head, seeing darkness and feeling the wind fling points of snow into his face. The moon was gone, clouded over or set, and the world beyond the overhang of rock was of a shimmering near-black and without form.

Isham was still out there, he thought, but there was damn little chance of finding him without light. But that worked the other way around, too. Ish wasn't likely to take a chance on trying to sneak up in the darkness. Not against an armed man he couldn't see, certainly not when he wasn't sure he couldn't be seen or heard. No, he'd settle down to wait for dawn.

"Sheriff?" Clant said in reply as he moved himself toward Glynn. Lady was dead, but the sheriff wasn't. He had to do what he could to help Glynn.

He didn't dare strike a light. That would be a sure guide for Isham. With his fingers, he examined Glynn's leg.

"Goddamn fool thing," the sheriff said painfully. "I took the damn bullet clean enough and then busted the bone coming off my horse."

"Been worse if the ball had busted it," Clant muttered. The sheriff had managed to do well enough for himself. He'd scraped enough cobwebs to plug the

131

bullethole in his thigh and stop the bleeding. And he'd gotten himself out of the wind under shelter of the overhang.

"Break feels clean," he told Glynn. "Didn't come through the skin. I might could set and splint it. It'll hurt like hell if I try, though."

"Try," Glynn said.

"Need sticks."

"There's some in here. I felt 'em when I come in. Firewood, I think. Like somebody'd made camp here some time or another."

Clant felt around in the darkness until he found the little pile of branches. It wasn't much, but it was the best he had. He felt through them, sorting out the ones that would do.

"Wish to hell we could start a fire," Glynn muttered as he returned with the sticks.

"Yeah." Clant busied himself gathering the material he'd need. Hesitantly, he took a petticoat from the body of the girl. "It ain't a proper thing to do," he muttered. "But I reckon she'd of understood."

He shredded it into strips. When he had the pieces laid out where his hands could find them, he took hold of the sheriff's ankle. He said grimly, "You holler loud enough to be heard over that wind and we're both dead, you know."

Glynn didn't holler.

When it was done, with the last knot cinched tight, Clant sat back on his haunches and wiped the sweat off his face. He felt washed out, downright exhausted, and he wondered how Glynn felt. He asked.

It was a long moment before the sheriff answered, and when he did his voice was weak and strained. He said, "Thirsty."

132

Clant moved toward the mouth of the shallow cave and felt the ground. The snow was coming down plenty hard now, laying a blanket on the grass. He rubbed his hands in it and wiped them down his pants legs. Then he scooped up handfuls of the fresh-fallen snow for the sheriff. He took a mouthful himself, letting it melt and trickle down his throat. It felt good, even if it was damn cold.

When he'd done what he could for Glynn, he started searching with his hands for the Colt he'd dropped. He found it and settled against the wall of the cave, punching out the spent cartridges and replacing them.

"A right nice gun," he muttered as he stuffed it into his waistband.

"Ought to be for the price," Glynn said. His voice sounded a fair bit better now.

"How you feel?"

"Pain's eased off enough I've begun to notice I'm freezing."

Clant nodded. He dug into his pocket for the Dan'l Webster. "Chaw?" he asked.

"I'll try anything once."

He held the plug for the sheriff to bite off a piece; then he gnawed a quid himself.

"Damned stuff bites back, don't it?" Glynn mumbled.

"Does it? I ain't noticed."

"How long you been chawing this poison?"

"Hell, I ain't recall that far back. Since sometime when I was a kid."

"It's a damned poor substitute for a cigarette," Glynn said, and then spat.

Clant worked the quid and told him, "Bad habit, smoking."

He heard Glynn snort and then ask, "Why you say

133

that?"

"Mainly the fire. Times like now, a man can't light a fire. Not when he's hid in the dark. He can't dare show a match or the glow of the ash and he can't put the smell of burning tobacco in the wind. If he's holed up the way we are, he just plain can't smoke." He fingered what was left of the plug and added, "Cigarettes is a nuisance, too, with all them pieces—loose tobacco and papers and matches. And a man's got to make his quirly afore he can use it. Ol' Dan Webster, though, he's a real fair friend. Man can chaw on the run and spit on whoever's chasing him. 'Sides that, chawin'll ease his thirst."

"I never thought about it that way," Glynn said. "Ain't often I'm on the run."

"I'd sooner not be."

After a long moment of silence, the sheriff spoke up again. "Dammit, I can't hold off no longer. What the hell we messed up in, Clant? Who's that out there shooting? Fairweather?" It was in his voice that he'd been waiting, hoping Clant would open up without his having to ask, and he sounded embarrassed about finally breaking down and putting the question to him.

"My brother Isham," Clant said. "Him and Fairweather got a notion they couldn't trust me no more. Only Lady got me loose. And I got her killed." He gazed into the darkness, listening to the howl of the wind.

"I had my sights on him once there," he said softly, as if he were talking to himself instead of the sheriff. "I let him go. If I ain't had done that, he couldn't have killed her."

"That's Isham out there gunning for you?" Glynn sounded as if he couldn't quite believe it.

"I should have killed him. I had my sights on him.

134

Maybe I ain't the man I figured myself to be."

"On account of you didn't shoot down your own brother? You can't fault yourself for not shooting at your own blood kin."

"Meldrin blood," Clant said, as if it were the answer. After a while he asked, "You recollect I had a brother Bob? He was oldest boy. Died back afore that ruckus in Bloomington."

Glynn recalled the eldest of the Meldrin brood, a broad-shouldered, red-bearded young man with a quick, vicious temper. He mumbled, "I recollect him."

"Wasn't nobody but Pap himself that shot down Bob."

"What?"

"Yeah," Clant said slowly. "Bob had took to acting up. He had started talking at the rest of us how Pap was getting too old. Said we needed a younger, faster man to lead up things. After we'd made such a mess of robbing that bank in Rennert we went back home to rest up and make new plans. Bob, he kept pulling us into corners and talking at us.

"Pap knew about it all right, but he never said nothing. Not till one night we'd all set down to the table for supper. Real quiet-like, Pap drawed his gun and give Bob three slugs in the gut, right under the table. Then he stood up with the gun in his hand and said, 'They's three more balls in this here revolver. Anybody else got any ideas about who's head of this family?'

"Wasn't nobody spoke out again' him so he explained to us how we was all Meldrins and we had to stick together on account there sure as hell wasn't nobody else gonna stand up for none of us. After that he loaded up the empty chambers and then we et."

He pulled the plug out of his pocket and took another

bite of it. Then he said, "That's what was in my mind when I got my sights on Isham—how Pap'd shot Bob. Only when I drawed back the hammer I got to thinking how they wasn't none of us Meldrins left now exceptin' Isham and me. For all of his hollering and chasing after me, I couldn't think but that he was my brother and how we had to stand together on account they wasn't nobody else would stand up for none of us."

It was a long while before Glynn asked, "What are you going to do?"

"Ain't nothing I can do now," Clant answered. "Got to wait till there's light. Then I reckon I'm gonna find him and kill him."

The wind died down a little before dawn, but the snow was still falling hard when the sky began to change from a flat black to a dull lead gray.

Clant checked over both guns. He had five loads left in the Remington. Pulling off the gunbelt, he handed it and the Colt to Glynn, saying, "Maybe I ain't come back. Maybe you'll need this."

"I need *you*," the sheriff answered. "I can't get out of here alone."

"No, not alone," Clant muttered thoughtfully. Then he said, "Can't neither of us get out of here long as Isham's outside waiting to get his sights on us."

He stepped to the mouth of the cave. The way the snow was coming down, he couldn't see more than a few long strides ahead of him. He ducked out, keeping close to the rocks. Isham might have moved during the night, might have tried sneaking in closer. It was fair likely Ish had a good notion of about where he'd been holed up and was just waiting for enough light to make his move. His back against the rock, he called out,

"Brother Isham!"

There was no answer. But with the wind almost stilled, he could hear the crunch of snow under boots. He tried to figure the direction and distance. Not too far and just a bit over to his left. With the revolver cocked, he stepped out from his shelter and called again, "Brother Isham!"

This time he drew fire. Two shots, snapped off as quick as a Colt could throw them. It had worked—his sudden appearance had gotten Ish excited.

He'd seen the flame of the gun. Ish was up behind and against a boulder, close enough for him to see the shape of it through the snow. And close enough for Isham to see him. He had to keep Ish too flustered to steady up his gun.

Bringing the Remington up, leveling it toward the rock, he began walking. He had five loads, and he couldn't afford to waste them "Maybe you're right, Brother Isham," he called.

Ish fired, two more quick, nervous shots.

Clant walked toward him. He could see Isham's hand now, with the gun in it, thrust from behind the rock. He could see Ish inch his head out, trying to sight along the barrel of the Colt. He was close enough to look into his brother's face.

"Maybe you're right. Maybe I been no-account and shiftless and maybe you ain't can trust me," he said, his voice holding steady as he looked back down the barrel of the Colt. He could see Isham's puzzlement. He added, "But you got to own I got a good hand on a gun."

He held the Remington level and squeezed at the trigger. The hammer began its long, slow fall. It hit with a dull, dead click on a bad cap.

Clant was still walking forward as he thumbed the hammer back again. He felt Isham's bullet slam across his side, twisting him, staggering him back, but he managed to keep his feet. He leveled the Remington, closing his finger on the trigger.

The Colt in Isham's hand spit flame again and Clant felt the slug ram like a cannonball into his shoulder. It hit hard, jerking his arm back as the hammer touched the cap. The powder exploded, sending the ball wild into the air. At the same time the gun bucked itself out of his hand.

He saw it land in the snow and he started toward it. The pain ran out from his shoulder, through his whole body. His legs didn't want to move. But he could see Isham fumbling at the loading gate of Colt with ice-stiff fingers.

Awkwardly, Clant dropped to his knees to reach for the Remington. There was no feeling in his left arm now and only a dull throbbing pain in his side. The arm didn't seem like a part of him. He managed to get his hand over the butt of the gun. His fingers dripped blood onto it and onto the snow around it. He knew he was touching it but there was no feeling in his fingertips. He tried to grasp it but his hand wouldn't move.

He looked up at Isham, bent over the Colt anxiously working the ejector and Ish looked back. Seeing him there, on his knees, spilling his blood on the snow, Ish grinned and called to him, "Without that gun hand you ain't no goddamn good at all, little brother."

There were three loads left in the Remington, Clant thought as he reached for it with his right hand. His eyes touched the ragged scar on his wrist and he remembered all the times that hand had been useless to him. Feeling the fear strong in him, he tried to close his hand on the

138

butt of the gun.

The fingers moved, wrapping around it. The forefinger slid onto the trigger, and the thumb settled against the hammer.

Catching his breath, he looked toward Isham and slowly raised the revolver.

He saw Ish let back the gate and lift up the Colt. Under his own thumb, he felt the tension of the Remington's hammer. He wanted to slip it—bring it back almost to cock and let it fall and fire. But the feeling in his right hand—his judgment of the strength of it—was bad. He suddenly felt the hammer catch in the notch and hold at cock. Cursing himself, digging his teeth into his lip, he ordered his finger to close on the trigger.

Nothing happened.

For a goddamn long time nothing happened. Isham stood as if frozen, with the Colt raised up and leveled. Then—suddenly—Clant felt the gun in his hand buck. He saw surprise on Isham's face and he saw the small hole appear in the front of Isham's shirt.

Ish stepped back, a slow uncertain step. He bent a bit, and then began to fold up. The Colt went off as it slid out of his fingers, throwing a slug straight into the snow and following it down. It seemed to fall slowly and land gently.

Isham fell on his face on top of it.

Clant let the caught breath out of his lungs and drew another. It had all happened so slowly—then he realized that it had not been slow at all, but that his thoughts had raced so that the things he had seen had seemed to hold like the flow of cold molasses. His hand had obeyed him. His finger had closed on the trigger. And brother Isham was dead.

But it wasn't done yet. Glynn was still back there in that hole and Nora Ellison was still waiting in town for the promise Clant had given her.

He stuffed the Remington back into his waistband and worked the fingers of his good hand under his shirt. The slug had cut a ragged gash in his side but it wasn't deep. To the bone maybe, but not through it. Likely the rib was cracked. He couldn't tell for sure. But there wasn't any question about his shoulder. That bone was sure as hell busted.

Both wounds were spilling out his blood and he could feel a dull throbbing with the beating of his heart. The way the blood ran from his side, it wouldn't matter whether the bone was busted or not if he didn't get it stopped pretty quick.

He gathered a handful of snow and packed it against the wounds. It would stay the bleeding, maybe stop it completely.

It numbed the throbbing too. And after a moment, he struggled onto his feet. His head felt God-awful light and it was hard to make his legs move. He set his mind to it. Head down against the falling snow, he began to walk back toward the cave.

It was a long way, a damn long way. But finally he was there, dropping himself down to the ground at Glynn's side.

"You hurt, Clant?" he heard the sheriff say. The voice sounded far off.

"No," he said, his own voice sounding strange and distant to him. He leaned his head back, and rested it against the wall of rock. Softly, he said, "Isham's dead."

Glynn asked something else but he couldn't make it out. Then he heard himself say, "I ain't can make it, Sheriff. I ain't can walk as far as town afoot."

If Glynn said anything else he didn't know about it. He sat there for—he wasn't sure—it seemed like a long time. His eyes had closed and when he realized it and forced them open he had a notion he'd been asleep. His side was throbbing again but there was no feeling in his arm at all. And no pain, only the numb cold.

He raised his head and looked at Glynn. The sheriff was lying quiet, watching him.

"Clant, how bad are you hurt?"

He considered as he dug his right hand into his pocket for the plug. He got a chaw off it and worked his jaws a while before he answered, "Not bad. Just weak. Reckon I lost some blood. Maybe I sleep a mite more, I could set out for town."

"Like hell." The sheriff shook his head. "You wouldn't make it. You'd end up dead out there in the snow."

"I ain't think so," Clant muttered. He let his eyes close again. "I ain't know 'lest I try."

"Like hell," Glynn mumbled.

Clant frowned. He asked, "You hear anything, Sheriff?"

Glynn listened too. "Horse?" he suggested.

"Maybe. Maybe more'n one. If there is a horse coming likely it's Fairweather." Clant listened for another moment. "Maybe he got to wondering about Isham and come to hunt for him. Likely he heard the shooting."

Wrapping his good hand around the butt of the Remington, he moved himself to the mouth of the cave and peered into the falling snow. He could see them, three dark blurs moving slowly.

He looked at the broad stains of blood on his sleeve and then turned toward Lady's body. It was awkward,

141

working the short coat off her with only one hand. It was even harder forcing his arm through the sleeve and then getting the other sleeve on. But he had to cover the wounds.

As he scrubbed the dried blood off his left hand with a fistful of snow, he asked, "Glynn, you got hold of that Colt revolver?"

The sheriff nodded and closed his fingers around the gun's butt. He suggested, "Maybe they'll miss us."

"I mean to make sure they ain't miss us," Clant said. "We need a horse. You cover me but don't shoot if you ain't have to. Don't let 'em know you're here."

Taking up the Remington again, he got to his feet and headed into the snow.

CHAPTER 12

THE SNOW WASN'T COMING DOWN AS HARD AS IT HAD been, but it still thickened the sky. It had already begun to bury the body of Isham Meldrin when Clant reached the rocks where his brother had fallen.

Leaning his back against the rock, bracing himself to stay on his feet, Clant looked down at the body. If it hadn't been Ish, he told himself, it would have been him. It still might be. Through the screen of snow, he could see the three men on horseback. With his arm covered by the jacket, he thought, with luck they wouldn't realize he was hurt.

But he *was* hurt. His gun hand was useless. And right-handed he'd be damned lucky to have any control over the gun at all. He might be able to fire it but he sure as hell couldn't aim. His target would have to be so close he just plain *couldn't* miss.

"Fairweather!" he called out, "Over here!"

They heard and headed toward him. He could see the rifle Fairweather carried over the pommel of his saddle. But the other two, with their heads ducked against the snow, didn't seem to have bothered with drawing guns. Fairweather halted them with a gesture and eyed Clant.

"What happened?" he asked, his voice soft and mild.

"Isham run into a little trouble," Clant said. He let his right hand, with the cocked Remington in it, hang at his side, but he knew Fairweather saw the gun. The others saw it too, and looked at him curiously, but neither moved.

Narrowly, Fairweather asked, "What kind of trouble?"

"Me."

The outlaw lifted an eyebrow and Clant nodded toward the body. Stepping down off the horse, Fairweather headed over to it and nudged it with his boot. He toed it over onto its back. The face seemed to have frozen in that moment of surprise, the eyes wide.

In a smoothly quiet voice, Fairweather asked, "You coming back in with us, boy?"

"No," Clant answered. "'But I got business with you, *amigo*. My dun's up to your camp and I ain't expect I'll be getting back that way to fetch him. I want to trade you for one of these here horses."

He saw the subtle movement of Fairweather's hand on the rifle as the outlaw smiled and lied. "That sounds reasonable. But how come you won't throw in with us, Clant? There's money in it for you."

Clant felt the tension spreading through his body. What kind of a fool did Fairweather take him for, trying to distract him with talk that way? He wondered if Paul was fool enough to be possumed with talk. Slowly, he answered, "I reckon Isham was right about me, *amigo*."

He could see the puzzlement in Fairweather's icy blue eyes. "*No comprendo.*"

"You ain't can trust me no more, *amigo*. I still got that tin star in my pocket."

"What the hell you mean by that?" Fairweather jerked out the words.

Clant was grinning as he said, "You boys figure you're gonna ride into Jubilee like it was a picnic and just help yourselves to that bank money? You go into Jubilee and you'll be taking the shortline straight to hell." He chanced glancing toward the two riders. They were listening intently.

"Think of it, Paul," he continued. "A whole town just waiting for you, expecting you, and loaded for you. I been there once myself and I can tell you it ain't my idea of fun. A gun behind every door and on every roof and you're there in the middle without no way to run—"

"You goddammed double-crossing little—" Fairweather's hand swung up the rifle, triggering it. But not fast enough or far enough. Clant had jerked up the Remington, the muzzle close, the slug slamming into Fairweather, buckling him over.

"Goddammed double-crossing—" he repeated, trying to lever another shell into the chamber. He fell, sprawling over Isham's body.

Clant felt the spatter of chips as Fairweather's slug struck the rock near his knee. Wheeling, he waved the handgun toward the men on horseback. With a strange detachment, he wondered whether he could hit a thing as big as a horse at that distance, firing right-handed. He thumbed back the hammer, thinking maybe he was going to find out.

He knew these two men. Both were from southern

144

Texas; one was named Rufus and the other, some kin of his, was called Palmer. They were no kin of Fairweather's though. They owed him no blood debts. Clant looked from one to the other.

Neither had made a move.

"You fellers want to try?" he asked.

Rufus moved his gaze to the two bodies in the snow and then back to Clant. He knew the name of Meldrin well enough. Shifting uncomfortably in the saddle, he glanced at his cousin.

"To hell with it," he answered in a thick mumble. "Too damn cold up here. My hands is near froze."

"Palmer?" Clant said.

"I got nothin' personal again' you, Meldrin," the second man answered. "Hell, Paul was gettin' too damn big for his britches anyhow. He figured he knew everything."

"You reckon you could do better?" Clant asked.

Palmer nodded sullenly.

"Then maybe you'd want to take the boys on back south. Thaw out a mite and find yourself a nice fat bank to tackle. Only don't mess around Jubilee, though. Don't ever come back around these parts. You ain't like the climate at all. Too cold in the mountains and too hot down to town."

Palmer nodded again, "I don't hanker to try no town what knows I'm coming."

"That's good thinking. You just keep on thinking that way, you hear? You just keep in mind as how the law in Jubilee knows you boys too good to let you sneak up from behind," Clant told him.

He nodded.

Clant made a small gesture with the Remington. "Now you step down off them horses, both of you, and

145

head on back to camp else I change my mind."

Rufus climbed out of the saddle but Palmer hesitated, protesting, "It's cold for walking."

"It's even colder for getting buried."

Palmer moved, swinging his leg over the cantle and letting himself down off the horse. Moving with a stiff slowness, he joined his cousin and they started walking.

"Rufe," Clant called.

The man half-turned, looking back over his shoulder.

"You chaw, ain't you?" Clant asked.

Rufus nodded.

"Got any spare eatin' tobacco on you? I left mine up to the camp."

Rufus dug his chilled fingers into a pocket and came up with a plug. He gave it an underhand toss toward Clant.

"Obliged," Clant grinned. "Help yourself to mine when you get back to camp. Now, move."

He waited until they'd been lost from sight in the swirl of the snow. Then he thrust the gun into his waistband and forced his cold-stiff fingers off the butt.

Moving was hard. He had to get down onto his knees to pick up the plug of tobacco and then struggle up again to gather the reins of the horses. He led them back to the rock and looked down at the bodies. Snow was beginning to blanket Fairweather now, too.

He got himself onto his knees again and fumbled open the buttons of Fairweathers coat. The revolver in the dead man's holster was one of the new model Colts. It seemed like everybody was carrying them these days, he thought as he worked the belt buckle open. Leastways everybody who throwed a gun. Fairweather's would be a good one. Old Paul wouldn't settle for less than the best in firearms. But he wouldn't be needing it

146

anymore.

He pulled the belt from around the dead man's waist, but one-handed, he couldn't buckle it around his own. Getting the buckle closed, he looped the belt over one of the saddles. He'd sure got a notion to own one of those Colts.

He gathered the reins again and stumbled back toward the cave. It took the last of his strength to get there. Leaving the horses ground-hitched, he dragged himself in and dropped to the ground.

He wanted a chaw but he felt too tired to dig in his pocket for the plug. Wearily, he leaned his head back against the wall. His eyes didn't want to stay open, so he let them close. He could hear Glynn saying something but he couldn't make out the words.

"I got us some horses," he tried to tell the sheriff. But he couldn't make out his own words either.

When he opened his eyes again, he knew for sure that he'd been asleep this time. And it had done him good. He was still cold, still too numb to feel the wounds as more than a throbbing ache, but he could tell that he'd gotten back some of his strength. He wondered if he was strong enough to try moving out.

He sat a while longer, chewing tobacco and answering the questions Glynn put to him, as he thought it out. He couldn't leave the sheriff here alone while he headed toward town for help. For one thing he wasn't that certain he could make it himself. For another, the sheriff likely couldn't last it out alone and injured until help could get back from town. So Glynn had to be taken along.

He might be able to sit a horse, Clant figured, but it would likely cause him a fair lot of pain. And once the horse started to move, it could be nigh unbearable. But

Clant knew that even if he'd had the strength to rig a travois, there were parts of the trail down that it couldn't be hauled over. So Glynn would have to ride down, horseback.

He told Glynn his thoughts and the sheriff agreed. It might be damn hard, but it was the only way.

Clant planned it all out before he tried to move. The hardest part was getting Glynn onto the horse's back. Once he was there, wrapped in the saddle blanket Clant had stripped off the spare horse, he held on and helped Clant use the reins and latigos off the discarded gear to tie himself to the saddle.

Finished, Clant had to lean himself against the rocks again to stay on his feet. He'd run short of strength and the exertion had set his side to hurting. Despite the snow, there was sweat on his face. He wiped at it with the back of his hand and waited. Resting, he grew cold again and it eased the pain. Maybe it would do as much for Glynn, he thought as he dragged himself up onto the red roan that had been Paul Fairweather's own mount.

When he turned to check Glynn before he laid heels to the roan, he saw that the sheriff was slumped forward, his chin on his chest. He was asleep, or more likely unconscious, Clant figured. It was the best thing.

At first the roan was rambunctious. It didn't like the snow and wanted to head back to the outlaw camp. It kept him busy for a while and the sweat beaded on his face again as he played at the reins. But on the trail, with Glynn's mount following docilely and Clant's hand firm on the bit, the roan settled.

After that Clant realized that he was sleeping in the saddle himself. It was a thing he'd done often enough in his life, but he fought it now. Without a hand on the rein, the roan still might try to turn back. If not that, it

148

would likely try to stop and hunt graze or wander off the trail and drift. He had to keep it headed. And he had to get on to Jubilee as soon as he could—not just for the sheriff's sake, but for himself as well. He knew he needed food and warmth, maybe more. He damn well needed rest. As hard as he fought it, he couldn't keep himself awake.

He had no way of telling how long they'd been traveling. He was aware that the light faded, that night came, and that the snow stopped falling. He was aware that he'd wakened a number of times to kick the lagging horse back into motion and head it again.

Day came, gray and dull, but still he couldn't keep himself awake. His mind seemed to drift away from his body, leaving it too numb now even to feel the cold. He seemed to be in other places and other times—reliving things that had happened long before.

It was the wind-borne snow that brought him back to the present. It was flung stinging into his face. He got his eyes open and squinted against it There was ice in his hair and in the scruff of beard on his jaw. It caked over his hand on the reins where it had melted against his skin and then frozen again. His fingers wouldn't move. Winter had come onto Bloodyhead Mountain and had settled hard.

He tried to remember back to a time before the snow, before he had begun riding endlessly through it. From somewhere in the back of his mind he recalled Nora Ellison. He remembered a warm, dry kitchen with hot coffee in a cup in front of him, the steam rising into his face. He could damn near smell that coffee.

He blinked against the snow. It was dark. Night again? How long had he been riding? He couldn't be sure. He had no sense of time left.

He managed to get the reins looped around the saddle, horn and his hand thrust inside the coat against his body. He got the fingers to move and with them he dug the plug of tobacco out of his coat pocket. It seemed to be frozen, too. Finally he got a quid between his teeth. The tobacco helped. He got his eyes open again.

Something was showing in the darkness ahead. He squinted against the snow, trying to make it out. Light?

The dull glow formed itself into a yellow square, a lamplit window with the falling snow making a halo around it. And there were more lights. A house? A whole damn town!

The sight of it sent a shudder along his spine and kicked his brain to working again. He remembered the horse he'd been leading. It was still there, plodding. wearily along behind with the blanketed bundle still slumped where he'd tied it in the saddle.

He shoved his heels into the sides of the exhausted roan and headed it toward the lights. But they were beginning to blink out, one by one. For a long terrible moment he thought that the town was going to disappear like a dream and leave him alone in the snow. But not all of the lights went out. And the bulky shadows that were buildings held steady as he neared them. He sighed with relief. The lights were just being put out for the night.

As he rode into Long Street the horses came awake and smelled the air, eyeing the lanterns that still burned in front of a few of the buildings. There was a strong scent of hearth fires and a few windows still showed light, but the street seemed deserted.

Up ahead, Clant could see the sign that hung over the door to the sheriff's office. There seemed to be a light burning behind the window. He told himself that

150

somebody would be there minding the store. Somebody *had* to be there.

He dropped rein and swung stiffly out of the saddle. He managed to stay on his feet. For a long moment he stood there with the snow swirling around him and his face pressed into the horse's neck. The warm, pungent smell of the animal was familiar and it was good. It set him in mind of barns with stalls full of straw where a man could lie down and burrow in out of the cold. But he had something more to do before he could rest. He had to find someone to look after Lamar Glynn.

He straightened up and got himself a bite off the plug, knowing it would help. Then he started for the sheriff's office. It was a damn long way across the plank walk. He pushed the door open and leaned his good shoulder against the frame.

Johnny Ward sat at the desk, his feet up on it and a hat over his eyes. He jumped as the door slammed open.

Shoving the hat back, he started to holler; "Shut that damn door behind . . ." His voice trailed off as he squinted at Clant.

"Meldrin!" he said, making a sound almost like a question.

Clant heard his own voice, icy-hoarse. "Glynn's outside, tied in his saddle. You'd better look after him."

"What?"

"Quick," he added, and left it at that. He could feel his strength giving out and he knew he wouldn't be able to stay on his feet much longer. But damned if he'd fall on his face in front of Johnny Ward.

He took a step. And then another, walking toward the back room. He got himself in and clutched at the bars to support himself. The cell was still empty, still open. He managed to get as far as the cot.

Clant opened his eyes in darkness. All he could make out was the dull glow of a clouded night sky behind a tiny barred window.

Prison?

For an instant he panicked at the thought. Then he remembered. This was the jail in Jubilee.

He lay there, recalling what he could, trying to sort the bits of dream from the things that were real. He was on a cot and under blankets, stripped to the waist but warm enough. His right hand explored the bandages. From the feel of the adhesive plaster cinched around him, he did have a busted rib. And the broken arm was strapped down tight, with his hand in a sling. At least he still had the hand, he thought as he ran his fingers over it. It didn't feel swollen or anything like that. Maybe the wound had been clean.

He had a vague memory of a doctor and of pain. He seemed to recall the doctor assuring him the arm would heal. He had a funny recollection, too, of the doctor trying to order him out of the jail cell and of himself insisting that if anybody had a right to a jail cell, he did. But maybe that memory belonged with the dreams.

He stirred himself a bit, trying to get as comfortable as he could, and he let his eyes close again. He slept soundly this time, without dreaming. And when he woke again, it was daylight. Beyond the small window he could see the crisp, clear blue of the sunlit sky. In the air he could feel a chill that suggested there was snow lying on the ground. He remembered how he'd meant to travel south before the snows came. And he remembered how, a long time ago it seemed, he'd bought a horse to make the trip on. That plan had sure gone to hell the quick way.

He tried sitting up. It wasn't too hard. He felt weak and a little dizzy but not really bad. He leaned his elbow on his knee and rested his chin in his good hand. For a while he sat there, gazing at the open cell door and trying to recall what had happened since he had gotten back from the mountain. He had a strong feeling that more than one night had passed.

Looking around the cell, he got to wondering where his coat with the Dan Webster in the pocket might have gotten to. He could recall somebody slashing his shirt to pieces to get it off him. He sure hoped the coat hadn't been taken off the same way—especially not with winter here and damn near everything he owned left at the outlaw camp.

He found his boots at the foot of the cot and worked them on. Standing up made him dizzy again, but the feeling passed and he decided he was capable of walking. The door into the sheriffs office was open, and even before he stepped through it he could feel the warmth thrown off by the big iron stove.

He stopped in the doorway, leaning his good shoulder against the frame, and looked at Lamar Glynn. The sheriff was sitting at the desk, studying a batch of papers.

It took Glynn a minute to realize he was being watched and look up. Frowning, he asked, "What the hell are you doing on your feet?"

"Looking for a chaw. Seems I recall I had a plug in my pocket." Clant spotted the coat hung from one of the wall pegs and headed for it. As he moved his head spun again and he had to brace himself against the wall for a moment.

"You better sit down before you fall down," the sheriff said.

"Yeah," he mumbled. Hauling the coat off the hook, he settled himself in the Windsor chair and spread it over his knees. He dug his hand into the pockets until he'd found the plug. When he'd gnawed off a quid, he leaned his head back against the wall and eyed the sheriff.

"Glynn, you up and around?" he asked.

"Like a damn three-legged calf." The sheriff jerked his thumb toward a pair of crutches propped in the corner behind him. "You did a good job with that splint."

"I done similar for my brother Asa once," Clant muttered. After a moment, he asked, "How long we been down off that mountain?"

"Little better'n a week."

"A week? Where the hell I been all that time?"

"On your back with fever. Mostly out of your head," Glynn told him. "You been pretty sick."

Clant let fly a spate of tobacco juice at the cuspidor. At least he wasn't too weak to spit straight. "I been sick afore, but never no week's worth," he said. "Only once I was ever down so far I couldn't haul myself onto a horse and move if I had to. And that was lead poisoning."

"The Bloomington raid?"

"Yeah." He spat again and wiped his mouth with the back of his hand.

"Do you get tobacco in the penitentiary, Clant?" Glynn asked.

"They give you a ration if you behave yourself. Which I generally didn't," he answered. "You want more, though, you can lay hands on it."

"How's that?"

"Meet the price. For a price you can get nigh

anything. Man learns the value of money in prison. The prices are right high, though. Thing a man inside needs is he's got friends outside what'll do for him." Clant looked at what was left of the plug. Then he looked at the sheriff and asked suspiciously, "Why? You got some notion you've got a charge again' me?"

"Should I have?"

That was a hell of an answer. He shifted uncomfortably in the chair and asked, "You ain't can hold me for hanging around with Fairweather, can you, Sheriff?"

Glynn shrugged and said, "Clant, you still got that deputy's badge I gave you?"

Clant nodded. He ran his hand through the pockets of the coat again, mumbling, "I got it here somewheres."

"You took an oath on that badge, Clant," Glynn said. "You were carrying it for me when you rode up to Fairweather's, weren't you? Whatever dealings you had with Fairweather up there, you were working for the law at the time, weren't you?"

"I sure ain't gonna argue you none on that," Clant said. He found the star and set it down on the corner of the desk.

Glynn eyed it. "You quitting me, Clant? Gonna run out again? Ain't you got the guts to stay here now and face up to an honest job?"

"What the hell you mean by that?"

"I mean if you still want this job, you still got it. But I'm warning you, if you work for me you'll *earn* your wage. You'll damn well learn to behave yourself and respect the law. You understand?"

Clant bit another chunk off the plug and worked at it a while. Then he looked at the sheriff again and said, "You figure you got me in another wolf trap, Glynn?"

"Huh?"

"You reckon you can just keep talking at me till you've put a mess of damn mean thoughts into my head, ain't you? You figure if I up and pack out now, I'll all the time be thinking maybe you're right—maybe I ain't man enough to face up to it."

"Well?" Glynn grunted.

Clant picked up the star and ran his finger along the edge of it. "S'pose I did stay, what I have to do?"

The sheriff eased back in his chair and gave a sigh of satisfaction. He managed to keep a grin off his face as he said, "Not much. Just take orders during working hours. Lay off using your fists, except in the line of duty. Quit spitting on the sidewalks. You reckon you could handle it?"

"Well now, I ain't know," Clant drawled. "But then a man ain't never know what he can do till he tries, is he?" Fumbling a bit, awkward with his right hand, he pinned the star onto his coat.

We hope that you enjoyed reading this
Sagebrush Large Print Western.
If you would like to read more Sagebrush titles,
ask your librarian or contact the Publishers:

United States and Canada

Thomas T. Beeler, *Publisher*
Post Office Box 659
Hampton Falls, New Hampshire 03844-0659
(800) 818-7574

United Kingdom, Eire, and
the Republic of South Africa

Isis Publishing Ltd
7 Centremead
Osney Mead
Oxford OX2 0ES England
(01865) 250333

Australia and New Zealand

Bolinda Publishing Pty. Ltd.
17 Mohr Street
Tullamarine, 3043, Victoria, Australia
(016103) 9338 0666